Also by Alex Shearer

A MESSAGE TO
THE SEA

Also by Alex Shearer

The Cloud Hunters
Sky Run
The Ministry of Ghosts

A MESSAGE TO THE SEA

Alex Shearer

HOT
KEY
BOOKS

First published in Great Britain in 2016 by
PICCADILLY PRESS
80–81 Wimpole St, London W1G 9RE
www.piccadillypress.co.uk

ISBN: 978-1-8481-2569-8
also available as an ebook

1

Printed and bound by Clays Ltd, St Ives Plc

Piccadilly Press is an imprint of Bonnier Publishing Fiction,
a Bonnier Publishing company
www.bonnierpublishingfiction.co.uk
www.bonnierpublishing.co.uk

Yes, he thought, anyone could put a message in a bottle and throw it into the sea. There was nothing so unusual about that. But when the sea started writing back to you – that was different, that was special, that was weird and strange and wonderful. And even a little terrifying.

PROLOGUE

At the beach one day, Tom Pellow took a message he had written, and he put it inside a bottle. He screwed the top back on to the bottle, to make it watertight, and he threw it as far away as he could, into the sea.

The timing was good, for the tide was retreating, and the waves carried the bottle out towards the horizon. He saw the bottle bobbing away, moving amongst the breakers and foam, threading its way past the seaweed and kelp. There weren't many people around. Not a single surfer that afternoon. Just a couple of trawlers coming in to port, and some fishermen, in small boats with outboards, and a crabber, pulling in traps. Then he lost sight of the bottle. Next, he heard his older sister calling his name and saying that it was time to go home.

Tom thought about the bottle a few times after that, and wondered if anyone would find it. In a week or two, he had almost forgotten it. But, on occasion, it would come back into mind – on other walks along the coast, or when he saw an empty, discarded bottle lying by the pebbled shore.

But he didn't hold out much hope of anyone ever finding the message in the bottle. The world was a huge place and the ocean was the biggest part of it. The vast sea was immense, and his bottle was tiny. A whale might have swallowed it; a shark may have eaten it. It could have struck the hull of a boat, broken up and sunk. The message would be paper pulp, a ball of mush, soon to disintegrate and sink to the seabed.

That was what he thought had probably happened to it.

But no. It turned out that he was wrong.

1

DEAR FINDER

They had been in his mother's car, heading for the supermarket, when the song came on the radio. She obviously knew the lyrics, as she started to sing along with it, but Tom had never heard it before. It was catchy though, with a memorable tune. It was something about a message, and something about a bottle, and how a lonely man stranded on a desert island sent an SOS out to the world.

'Who is that?' Tom asked her.

'The Police,' she said.

He raised an eyebrow.

'The police?' he laughed. 'In a band?'

'No, not police*men*. The Police. That's the name of the group.'

'The Police?'

'Yes.'

He looked at her doubtfully. But his mother wasn't in the habit of lying to him, so he supposed he'd have to believe her. It was a funny name for a band though. Why not The Army? Or The Navy? Or The Traffic Wardens?

But it wasn't a bad idea, to send an SOS to the world. It needn't even be an SOS. It could just be *Hi!* It could be *Hello, how are you? What's happening where you are?*

All you needed was a pen and paper and a bottle. It would cost next to nothing, a thing like that. Tom's dad had said something to him about a message in a bottle once too, Tom remembered. He'd said how he'd thrown one into the water, and had had great hopes for it, back when he was a boy. But that, of course, was all a long time ago, and he'd never got a reply. And even if one came for him now, after all these years, it would arrive too late.

Tom spent some time composing the message. It wasn't easy. After all, who were you writing to? You had no idea. No idea at all whom the recipient of that message might be. You were writing to a stranger, who might not even speak your language, or, at least, not very well. Best keep it simple, in that case. Though that didn't make it any easier to write. Harder, if anything.

At home in his room that evening, Tom tore a sheet out from his notepad.

Dear Bottle Rescuer, he wrote.

Was that a good start? Maybe not. Too bland. He crossed it out.

Dear Rescuer of the Bottle.

2

No, maybe not that either – too dramatic.

Dear Sir or Madam.

No, no. Too formal. It sounded like he was writing to complain about something.

Dear Reader.

No, it wasn't right. Not quite.

Dear Finder.

Hmm. Maybe. Yes. That might do.

Dear Finder.

Now what?

Dear Finder,
My name is Tom and I live in a place called
Delwick, which is a small fishing village by the
sea.

Good start, he thought. Better not put in too much information though. You had to keep it short. You couldn't stuff your life story into a bottle. It was only supposed to be a message, after all. 'A message in a bottle', that was the expression. Not a novel in a bottle, or an essay in a bottle, or an illuminated manuscript in a bottle. Just a plain and simple message – short and to the point.

Tom felt as if he ought to have something important to say, but it was hard to think of what. Peace to the world, or save the whale, or down with global warming

– but everyone said that. And you certainly didn't need other people to tell you that kind of thing. You could think of all that for yourself.

All right, nothing too serious then. Something more personal.

Dear Finder,
My name is Tom and I live in a place called Delwick, which is a small fishing village by the sea. If you look it up in an atlas or on Google Maps you will no doubt find it and might even see some pictures.

The radio was on in my mum's car today and I heard a song about a message in a bottle and thought it might be fun to try it for myself. So this is it. I thought it would be interesting to see if anyone would ever find my message, and if so, where they would live and where the bottle would turn up and how someone would come to find it.

I dare say that you might even live in a different country and that this bottle – when you find it – may have been halfway round the world. Or even all the way round.

I don't expect an answer in a hurry, as I know that it can take months for bottles in the sea to be found – even years – assuming they are ever found at all.

4

I might try another bottle as well as this one. I might even try a bottle a week, as, let's face it, there is no shortage of bottles in the world, more like too many, if anything. So, if, by some chance, you find two bottles together, saying more or less the same thing and with the same name at the bottom of the message, you may discover that they are both from me. If so, it's because I have decided to send more than one message off after this one, as I said, and two of them have ended up in the same spot, though that would be quite a coincidence, I think, don't you?

Now that Tom had got started, he felt it easier to go on. He felt himself getting into quite a chatty mood.

I am going to write very small, he continued, *so I can write more, and I will use both sides of the paper. Hope it doesn't make it hard to read, as sometimes, when you write on both sides, the ink shows through on the other one. But I shall try to avoid that, if possible. I can't use a lot of bits of paper as they won't all fit in the bottle.*

If you want to know a little about me, well, I am still at school and live with my mum and my sister. My dad was a merchant seaman on a big container ship, but he was lost at sea a year ago.

5

My grandad was lost at sea too, not long after I was born, so I hardly knew him, but I have some photographs.

My grandad was a trawlerman and also a volunteer at the lifeboat station and that was how he was lost at sea, trying to rescue the crew of a stricken ship which had crashed on to the rocks. There are dangerous rocks near Delwick, called the Black Rocks, and even though there is a lighthouse it can still get very foggy and there have been many terrible shipwrecks over the years.

My dad was on a big container ship that overturned in bad weather and went down with all hands. This was far away in the Pacific, which is thousands of miles from here.

Life is hard on the sea, but I would still like to sail on it. But I guess I will have to think about that first, as it would be hard on Mum if I went too, after everything that has happened, and I think she'd rather I stayed away from ships and trawlers. So maybe I'll have to do something else, a dry land sort of life and a dry sort of job. But it's a pity as I see the sea every single day and I like it – stormy or calm. I could watch the sea for hours and not get tired of it, for it's always moving and when I watch it, I feel restless too, *just like the waves, and you can understand why people want to travel, when you live next door to the sea.*

I guess that you must live by the water too or you would not have found this bottle – unless you are on your holidays, of course.

Anyway, my email address is at the bottom of the page, so you can write back to me that way, if you like. Or, if you want to be adventurous too, you could try a message in a bottle as well.

Wouldn't that be something – if you found my message in a bottle and then sent out one of your own and I found your reply? What would be the chances of a thing like that ever happening? And yet, if it did, how cool would that be? That would be incredible, don't you think?

So I'll sign off now. Whoever you are and wherever you may be, I wish you luck and say hello. Best wishes to you and to your family, if you have one, and if you don't it doesn't matter and a big hello anyway. Maybe you are a lonely mariner out on the sea or a single-handed sailor going round the world. Write back if you can and if you want to. We can even be bottle friends, which is a bit like penfriends only with bottles.

I'm going to roll this up now and put it in the bottle and screw the stopper tight so that it won't leak and so the ink won't run. And then I'm going to go down to the beach and throw the bottle into the sea.

Hope to hear from you one day soon – or if not soon, then whenever.

Your message in a bottle friend,
Tom Pellow

And there, it was done. The message was written. Now it was just a matter of posting it.

2

BREAD UPON THE WATERS

You had, of course, to be reasonable. You couldn't expect a reply immediately. No way. You couldn't even expect an instant reply to an email, or to a text message, or to a tweet, or anything. Sometimes you couldn't even get an immediate reply from someone standing right in front of you, someone right there in the very same room. Like your sister, or your mother.

'Mum, can I go out down to the beach?'

Nothing. Silence. Blankness. Tom's mother was looking out of the window as if she hadn't heard. Or she had heard, but was distracted, her mind filled with other thoughts.

'Mum . . .'

'Sorry. Did you say something, Tom? I was miles away.'

He could guess who she was thinking of, and where those miles away had taken her. And if this was how it was with ordinary, everyday communication, then how was it going to be with a message in a bottle? How long did you have to wait for an answer? How

9

long should you delay before you went back down to the shore and started bottle spotting?

'Mum . . .'

'Yes, Tom, what was it?'

'Can I go down to the beach?'

'What for?'

'Just for a walk. Look at the boats. Look at the surfers . . .'

. . . Look to see if there's a bottle floating in on the tide, one with a reply in it, a response to my message.

'I suppose so. But be . . .'

Careful, of course. What else?

Tom stood at the shoreline, watching the eternally moving sea. It was never still, never satisfied; always restless, always moving, always coming in only to decide that it preferred to go back out again. And then, once out, back in it came. The water didn't seem able to make up its mind. It didn't know what it wanted at all. There were quite a few people like that – with their ever-changing moods.

There were half a dozen boats out, and some surfers, and someone in a canoe, and there were a couple of dog walkers on the beach today, their dogs off their leads and dashing into the waves, to be splashed and soaked, and then running back up the shore, shaking themselves, and with the water spraying from their backs in brief rainbows.

How long had it been? Tom wondered. Saturday, Sunday, Monday, Tuesday. Five days if you included today. Was that a reasonable length of time? Would someone have found the bottle by now? How far would it have travelled in five days? A mile? A hundred miles? A thousand? Halfway round the world? Maybe it had reached the equator and was already on its way back. Maybe he would be the one to find his own message? Wouldn't that be something? Wouldn't that be weird? Maybe a bit disappointing too.

Tom stared out to the grey sea. And it *was* grey today. Some days it was blue, others almost brown, when it churned up the sand. Sometimes it was green with algae blooms, and it could even turn black – dark and menacing, full of threat and force. Some days it was a sea to swim in, on others a place in which to drown – a sea to be avoided, to be afraid of.

He couldn't see anything floating out there – apart from the boats and the surfers chasing the waves, or waiting patiently for one to come their way.

Next time, Tom decided, he'd need to bring binoculars, or that old telescope which stood on the bookcase by the window. It had belonged to his grandfather.

Trouble with that though was that then people would know he was looking for something. They might start asking him questions, and a message in a bottle was a secret. It was a confidential matter, between you and the finder of the bottle. It was private, like a telephone call. You didn't want others listening in – or reading in. None of their business.

What if one of the surfers found it? Tom wondered. Would they hand the message over? It would be his by rights, but how could he prove that? He should have brought his own surfboard down and gone out on the waves himself. It was just a bit of a hassle sometimes, getting changed and putting on the wetsuit. You didn't always feel like going in. Some days it just looked too cold.

It was a fraught business all right, sending messages off in bottles. He wished he'd realised this before he'd started, how much stress there would be – the worry, the expectation, the hope, the disappointment, the resignation. The resignation to not getting an answer, that was.

Or maybe Tom would never be resigned to not finding a reply. He'd go on hoping and go on looking for a bottle floating in towards the shore until the day he died. Wherever in the world he ended up, however old he got, he would always go down to the sea, and look out for a bobbing bottle in the surf and the waves, and think, Is that my answer? Did someone find my message? Is that bottle meant for me?

12

Cast your bread upon the waters, for you will find it after many days.

Tom had heard that sentence used in church during a service and he hadn't really understood its meaning. Was it something to do with feeding ducks or seagulls?

But when he'd asked his mother, she had said that it was nothing to do with ducks at all. She'd said it wasn't to be taken literally. What it meant was that you should take a chance, that was all – be adventurous and be generous, without expecting a reward. It didn't mean that you should take a slice of bread or an old crust and chuck it into the sea. It just meant that you should take risks sometimes, and put your faith in luck and destiny and the higher powers, and then good things might come your way.

Well, what was the difference? Bread upon the waters, bottle upon the waters – wasn't it all part of the same thing? Wasn't throwing a message into the sea a hopeful act? One of faith and optimism? Tom felt it was. But to be on the safe side, maybe he shouldn't restrict himself to the one bottle, perhaps he *would* try a few more, like he'd planned. Just for insurance. After all, if you threw one slice of your bread upon the waters, well, that wasn't a great deal of dough. But if you tried a whole loaf of slices, that upped your chances, didn't it, of some kind of success?

Yes, Tom thought. That would be more positive,

more proactive. That would be far better than coming down to the shore every day and looking for a reply to his solitary message and not getting one. He should send out loads of messages, tons of them. The more he sent out, the greater his chances of one of them being found, and the greater his chances of getting a reply. Stood to reason.

'Stands to reason,' he heard himself say. 'That's what I've got to do. Get some more bottles.'

He walked off along the beach, hunting in the rock pools and the dunes, raking amongst the straggly seaweed and kicking up the pebbles, searching for bottles – proper bottles, that was, proper thick glass bottles of character and experience, ones that had knocked around a little and which were no strangers to the sea.

He could have used a bottle from home. There were plenty in the recycling box. But he didn't feel it would be right. His chances would be better with a beach-found bottle, one with fine scratches on its surface, smoothed and scarred by sand erosion, constant abrasion and the attrition of the weather.

Yes, that was the kind of bottle for him, an old sea faring, old sea dog of a bottle. One that had travelled and had stories to tell. Yes, he'd put his next message in a bottle like that, and then he would cast it far out upon the waters. Then he'd do another one.

He'd do a message a week, or even two messages

14

a week, or better still, a message every day. He'd send out hundreds of messages, that's what he'd do. He'd have his own army – no, *navy* – of bottles, his own fleet of bottles; Tom's messages in bottles, patrolling the seas, sailing around the world, bringing hope to castaways and succour to the lonely and delight to all those who found them.

He could be the bottle king. The emperor of all the messages in all the bottles. No one else had ever done that, had they? Or even thought of it. One bottle, maybe, yes, plenty of people tried that. But dozens of bottles, or hundreds, that was something different.

No longer downcast from not finding any reply floating in to him on the tide, Tom walked on, scouring the shoreline for new envelopes.

Glass envelopes. That was what a bottle was. It was a glass envelope. Only a stamp was not needed. Nor an address. Just a decent stopper to keep the wet out, and then you could post it. Postbox not needed either. The sea was his pillar box. Not red, admittedly, but his postbox just the same. Collections and deliveries at high and low tides. You just had to make sure you were there to pick up your mail. And, obviously, you had to spot it first.

Tom picked a piece of driftwood up and used it to poke and rummage in the sand and the seaweed. The tide was always bringing things in – ugly things, mostly:

bits of plastic, wrappers, bags, cartons, oil drums, containers. Once a month there was a tidy-up day, when local volunteers would turn up with sacks and pick up the debris. Keep Our Beach Clean was their motto.

But sometimes there was good stuff in amongst the trash. Sometimes there were expensive things. Especially after a shipwreck. Even big containers could drift in then, with all sorts of things inside them – motorbikes once, even, and another time carpets – and, once, thousands and thousands of tins of baked beans.

Everyone took some home – though they weren't really supposed to. It was beans until you were sick of them back then. It was beans until you never wanted to see a single bean ever again. Once it had been thousands of bottles of beer that had drifted in. Not that Tom had got any of that. One of the bottles would have been useful now though. Beer bottles were nice – brown and shapely, they'd make good envelopes. He might find one still, with a little luck.

Tom went on looking, unaware of the passing time. He never felt lonely, not down by the sea. He felt close to things there, and to people too – to his dad and his grandad, for that was where they were, there at rest somewhere at the bottom of the sea. The sea was their grave, their mausoleum. Dry-land people took flowers to cemeteries and laid them on the tombs of their loved ones. But people whose loved ones had

16

made their living from the sea and had perished upon it could not do that. There were no solid and permanent memorials for them. Moving sea and shifting sands were all they had.

He found a few plastic bottles, but they weren't what he wanted. It was proper glass ones he was after, bottles of character and substance and soul.

He was still looking when he heard his name being called.

'Tom! Tom!'

He looked up and in doing so he realised how dark it had become. His sister was standing at the breakwater, waving to him and calling his name.

'Tom – Mum says you're to come home now. You've to do your homework and dinner's ready.'

Tom did not immediately respond. Marie was all right, as sisters went, but the trouble with older sisters was they were just that – sisters, and older, usually thinking they knew more and knew better and were entitled to tell you what to do.

Since the loss of their father, Marie acted as if she were less of a sibling now and more of an additional parent. But Tom already had a mother, and no sister could take the place of your dad. Tom could look after himself – even if she did think otherwise.

'Tom! Did you hear? I don't want to have to ask you again . . .'

17

Don't want to have to ask you again . . . such a mum and dad kind of thing to say.

'Yeah, yeah, yeah . . .' he muttered. The wind carried his voice away.

'What did you say?' she called.

'Nothing.'

'Are you coming then?'

Once they had got up to mischief and had been conspirators. Now she had grown up and turned sensible. There was a distance between them. Why did she feel she had to look after him? For all she knew, he might be looking after her.

'Yes, all right.'

Reluctantly Tom turned and headed up the beach towards her. He hadn't found any usable envelopes, but he'd come back and look again tomorrow. Then he'd write another message and he would once more cast his bread upon the waters, just as the Good Book said, just as they said in church. *Cast your bread upon the waters, for you will find it after many days.* Or, with luck, somebody else might.

Someone would get back to him. He knew that. He knew they would. It was just a matter of faith, of believing. It was only a question of being patient, of waiting. The sea would take his messages away, and the sea would bring him answers. If you were patient,

Tom thought, all things would come to you – eventually, in the fullness of time.

'Are you okay, Tom?' Marie asked.

'I'm fine,' he said, his voice abrupt and surly.

She reached for his hand. Reluctantly, he let her take it. He was too old for all that now. All the same, he didn't squirm away, and they walked up the beach together.

3

ROSE HAVEN

Around the coast from Delwick harbour, going inland and upriver for a mile or two, was a wonderful and surprising sight.

No bridge had ever been built here, and the only way across that part of the estuary was on the *King Billy* ferry, which plied its way as slow and as regular and as interminable as clockwork. It ticked and it tocked across the river, back and forth, and forth and back, here and there, pendulum like, with nowhere else to go and no ambition to go there.

Tom's uncle, Gareth, was the captain of the *King Billy* ferry – he was Tom's mother's brother and Tom used to wonder, whenever he saw him, why Gareth hadn't yet gone mad.

Gareth should have gone mad by now. In fact, by rights, he should have gone mad several years ago. Or maybe he was mad already, in a sane-seeming kind of way. Perhaps he just didn't demonstrate any of the symptoms.

It was obvious to Tom why Gareth should have

gone mad, and yet nobody else seemed aware of it.

Gareth should have gone mad because all he did, all day long, each working day of his life, was to go back and forth across the river. He did it three times an hour. Loading and unloading the ferry with cars and passengers then crossing the river took twenty minutes. The ferry operated from eight in the morning until eight at night. Gareth crossed the river thirty-six times a day. He did this five or six days a week, and then a relief skipper gave him time off.

But even allowing for the days off, Tom's uncle should still have gone mad by now. Even allowing for his three weeks' holiday a year (and what did he do with that but go sailing?) he should still have gone mad. It was a miracle he hadn't – that or a testament to his steady nature.

Gareth was not the only one who should, by rights, be acting strange. There was also his crewman, Mike, whose job it was to wave the cars into place, and to collect the money from those making the crossing. Pedestrians paid a pound each and bicycles were free.

There were other ways over the river, but they were long diversions. It was ten miles upriver to the first bridge, and ten miles back down the other side to reach the ferry landing station on the opposite bank, which was really just a few hundred yards away. Had you not minded getting wet, and had your car been able to swim, you could have driven straight across in under a minute.

But even though Uncle Gareth's not going mad with the monotony of toing and froing across the same stretch of river all day was a remarkable thing, there was something even more remarkable than that in the vicinity.

Not that Gareth would have thought so, for it was a sight he saw thirty-six times a day. But for the first-time river crosser and ferry user, it came as a real surprise. It was as extraordinary as finding a hippopotamus in your bath. Your first thought would surely be – what is *that* doing there? It's got no business being there. It's in the wrong place, surely. It's lost its compass and gone astray.

Looking out from the ferry station by the bank, the river seemed quite ordinary. It was old and winding and full of bends. But halfway across, in mid-stream, what the curve of the river hid from the land was suddenly revealed.

There, close at anchor, no more than a quarter of a mile or so upriver, were two immense ships, temporarily at rest. They had been there a few weeks and might stay a few weeks more. And they were immense indeed. They were massive, ocean-going merchant ships, with main decks the size of several football pitches, and with towering tiers of further decks rising up to a dizzying height. They had huge funnels and sheer sterns and bows, rising like cliffs, and there were rope ladders, hanging like cobwebs, dangling down over their hulls, reaching as far as the water line.

Nothing could have seemed more incongruous than those two gigantic vessels at anchor in such a quiet, unobtrusive, unattended place. On the riverbanks were willows and ferns; there were swans on the water, and mallards and coots. But these boats had nothing to do with such fragile, freshwater things; they were something quite different, and separate somehow.

These were great cargo vessels that should have been plying their trade in the major shipping lanes of the world, filled with goods and minerals, with oil and iron ore, and a thousand other things. They looked as if they were hiding from someone here, like they were two ships on the run, holed up in a safe place, fugitives from the law.

The flags they flew were exotic and they bore the registration marks of far eastern states. Their crews were from everywhere – of every country, race and colour the world knows.

'Wow! What is *that*? What are they doing there?'

Uncle Gareth got asked that question twenty times a day – at least in summer, when the area was full of holidaymakers and their boundless curiosity and endlessly clicking cameras. But hearing, and then saying, the same thing over and over hadn't driven him mad either, no more than making the same short journey had.

'They're laid up at anchor,' he'd say. 'Not enough work for them at present. No cargoes to carry, so they're resting for now. Just for a week or three – couple of months at most.'

'Why here?'

'Perfect place,' Gareth would say. 'It's a haven – Rose Haven. Nice and quiet, like the name says. Out of the storms, out of the way. Berthing charges aren't much – not compared to what you'd pay at some busy port somewhere. They come from all over the world to park up here a while. They used to hide the navy here too, back during the war.'

'Is that so?'

'It is,' Gareth would tell the curious. 'Safe haven here. Safe as houses, ships are here. And it's not often ships are that safe. Nice deep water, calm and quiet. Do a little maintenance, keep a skeleton crew on board, and then, when things get busy and trade picks up and they have a cargo ready again, off they go.'

As he spoke, the ferry would carry on its way, and soon the great ships would disappear from sight – still there but hidden, back around the curve of the river, like slumbering, bleary-eyed giants, waiting for a roll of thunder or the banging of drums to stir them into action.

Gareth felt a little sorry for the men on board the waiting vessels. Often they wouldn't even be allowed off to visit the local towns and to stretch their legs on dry land. They'd remain on board, prowling the decks in their free time, or reading old paperbacks and watching DVDs. Sometimes the local chaplain would make a call, steering himself over in a small outboard, to climb the rope ladder and to enquire after the sea-farers' spiritual welfare. Or if anyone fell ill, a boat might take them for medical attention, or to have that throbbing tooth pulled out by the local dentist. But mostly the maintenance crews seldom got to leave their ships: their constant presence was required; or they were foreign nationals and the appropriate visas were lacking; or their passports were somehow missing; or their papers not quite in order.

When the big ships needed to sail, a couple of tugboats would be summoned. They would hitch up lines to the ships, and pull them along to get them started. The movement reminded Tom of elephants, and their great stubborn bulk, slowly shifting. The ships moved down to the river mouth on the high tide, and once there the tugs would untie their tow lines, and with hail-and-farewell toots of their funnel horns, they would see the cargo ships head out for deep water. And so the great boats would escape, like once beached and exhausted whales, now recuperated and returning to their natural element, liberated and churning the water.

What chance would a tiny bottle have against the steel hull of one of those huge vessels? Better than one would imagine, perhaps. The motion of the boat in the water would probably drive the tiny bottle away, bobbing off in its wake.

They floated in the same way too, the great and the small, the bottle and the tanker, all on the same principles of displaced water and trapped air. It was amazing the way that iron could float – steel too, and glass – just as long as you shaped it right. Objects that were heavier than water would float in it; and planes weighing tons could sail in the air.

With all those strange, seemingly impossible things going on, why not a message in a bottle too? Why couldn't that safely float elsewhere and be found, and maybe a reply make its way back again? Impossible things happened in the world every day and people took them for granted. So why not one more?

Sometimes, at weekends and during the long summer holidays, Gareth would let Tom come and help out on the ferry. Tom would collect the fares from the motorists, many of whom remained in their cars for the duration of the short journey. They missed the view of the huge container ships then, but what you don't know about you haven't really missed at all. The others, who decided to stretch their legs, were duly rewarded for their efforts.

Tom never worked for more than two days in succession. It wasn't that he minded helping, it was the tedium. Back and forth across the same stretch of river, thirty-six times a day. The only thing of interest to look at being the great cargo ships in the haven, and their skeleton crews.

These men, of all colours and all races, would be armed with rub-down sandpaper and paintbrushes and buckets and mops. Their work was to keep the metal-work spick and span and scrape off the ever hungry rust. Ships were always at war with corrosion and salt water. Tom both wished he was on board with them and was glad he wasn't. To be a merchant seaman and to sail all round the world was appealing, exciting, even romantic. But there was the downside too – the monotony, the maintenance, the battles with seaweed, sludge and barnacles. But then every great adventure had some dreariness to it somewhere.

'You ever think of a career on the sea, Tom? For when you grow up?' Gareth once asked him. 'Though I know your mother's firm against it. And for good reasons.'

'Sometimes,' Tom said. He wanted to add, 'Not a job like this though. Not back and forth on a flipping ferry all day. Not for me. No way.'

But he didn't really want to tell his uncle that he thought he had one of the most boring jobs in the world. He might take it personally. He'd probably be offended or angered.

It might even make him a bit mad.

4

MESSAGES TWO, THREE AND FOUR

A couple of weeks had gone by and as no replies had come to Tom's bottled message, he decided to send out a few more. The more the merrier, or, if not exactly merry, then the greater the chances of at least one of them being found. His patience with his first message had run out.

Tom sat in his room, pen in hand, a jotter in front of him. On his window sill were three bottles, all picked up from the beach, cleaned out and reclaimed.

One was an old cola bottle, one a beer bottle, the last a brown ginger-beer bottle, with a hinged top, made of a wire clamp and a metal and rubber stopper. No problems with sealing that one.

For the other two he had found a couple of corks, from amongst the crates and rubbish of the Anchor Inn and Public House down at the harbour. He had trimmed them with his penknife, and now they fitted fine. At least he hoped they would keep the water out for the duration of their journeys – however long and far that might be.

Now, the easiest thing would have been to write the same message again – identical to that put into bottle number one. But what was the point in sending off the same message repeatedly? Where was the fun in that? Surely someone who sends messages off in bottles could have a new identity every time? He could be whoever he wanted. One person today, another tomorrow. Who was to know? All the finder of the bottle could go on was the note inside. And, besides, Tom was in a somewhat frivolous mood.

Dear Bottle Finder . . .

Yes, good start, Tom thought. Now what? Who would he be this time? Not Tom Pellow again. That was boring. It was tedious to always be yourself. Better to be somebody else for a while. But who?

Ah yes. That would do. How about becoming an alien for a while?

Dear Bottle Finder,

I am an alien being from another planet, and I wish to communicate with you earthlings.

Now what? Oh, yes . . .

I come in peace. I have dropped this bottle into your ocean from a great height, from miles up in space, where I wait in my spaceship, along with plenty of food and a big flat-screen TV.

29

That would set the scene.

> *But this bottle is made of a special glass, unknown to earthlings, and it can withstand great temperatures, which is why it did not melt as it fell through your atmosphere, and is why it did not break when it landed in the water, even though it is like hitting concrete when you fall from a great height.*

You had to make it sound convincing.

> *I would communicate with you in person, only my appearance would be so frightening that you would probably wet your trousers if you ever saw me, and we aliens do not want you earthlings to do that, so we stay out of sight. We feel that to have wet trousers on a first meeting is not to get off to a good start.*

That added a nice touch of realism, Tom felt. He wrote on.

> *All the same, we wish to make contact with you, to warn you that you need to sort yourselves out a bit. You need to do something about global warming and all the litter on the beach. As aliens*

*of superior intelligence, we also have to tell you
that you give your school children far too much
homework to do and as a result you are burning
their brains out and giving them mental breakdowns – which could be easily avoided with less
homework and more pocket money.*

Yes. That might have some useful effect. Maybe one
of his teachers would find the message and pay a bit
of attention.

*We beseech you to learn the error of your ways
before it is all too late. If you do not do as we
instruct, we may have to land our spaceships and
take over your governments to make you do our
bidding.*

Nothing like a few threats to help things along.

*So, although we come in peace on the whole, you
had better not push your luck, as we are pretty
fearsome and very frightening-looking, as I said.
YOU HAVE BEEN WARNED.
Signed,
Zark of the Alien Brotherhood (and Sisterhood
as well).*

31

P.S. No need to reply to this message, but if you decide that you really want to, please reuse this same bottle, which can be recycled. You will have to throw it up into space very hard to get it into orbit and so will need strong arms. Or, better still, use a rocket if you have one. I suggest you look in the shed.

Tom put his pen down and read through his message with some satisfaction. Yes. He liked the sound of it. In fact he wished that he'd found a message in a bottle from an alien himself. It would be a good way for aliens to get in touch really. There might even be messages in bottles floating round outer space right now, just waiting for astronauts to find them.

He tore the sheet of paper from the notepad, rolled it up carefully, and inserted it into the cola bottle. Then he took one of the corks and twisted and banged it tightly into the neck. Then he set it aside.

Now then. Next letter. Next message. The one for the dark brown beer bottle. Who would he be now? Not another alien. Someone else, with a different kind of message for the world. He thought a while, then began to write,

Dear Finder of the Bottle,
I am writing to you to let you know that you

may have won millions and millions on the Message in a Bottle Lottery. In fact you may even have won squillions as well, but you need to check your number first. This is your number:

Tom thought for a moment then wrote: 9836983034389. He considered what to put next, then continued.

You will need to check your number on the Message in a Bottle Winning Number List, which you will find on the internet. Just use any search engine and input the words Message in a Bottle Lottery.

Once you have checked your number to confirm that you have won squillions, you just need to return your winning message to the sender – i.e. me.

Simply place a tick at the bottom of this message, next to the words: I am the holder of the winning Message in a Bottle Lottery number.

Add your name, address and telephone number, and confirm your identity by also adding the size of your shoes and how big your nose is.

Please Note: We will not be able to release your winnings until we have verified your shoe measurements and the dimensions of your nose. If you have big feet and an enormous hooter,

*you must not give false information, making out
you have a little hooter when you haven't. This
is crucial, so do measure it properly. If your nose
does not correspond to the measurements you
have given, you will not get your winnings.
Instead they will be given to charity, namely the
Old Dolphins' Home.*

*Once you have supplied the necessary infor-
mation, please re-cork this bottle and return it to
the sender at this address:*

The Top Bloke
Message in a Bottle Lottery Fund
The Far End of the Ocean
24, Somewhere or Other,
The Beach,
The Wet Place,
The World.
SEA 123

*We will get back to you as soon as possible,
but please do be patient, as it may take us some
time to receive your bottle – possibly a few weeks,
or even several thousand years. So do not hold
your breath in anticipation – not unless you are
really good at it and can go several years without
breathing.*

34

*Good luck with your claim and, if you have
won squillions, don't forget to share your good
fortune with others and to give a few quid to
charity. We suggest the Old Dolphins' Home
again, or if you would prefer to, why not donate
a few pounds to the Rest Home for Elderly
Kippers or to the Foundation for Orphaned Crabs
and Distressed Lobsters Who Have Fallen on
Hard Times? The Society for the Relief of Starfish
with Attention Deficit Disorders is also always
grateful for any help.*

*Goodbye for now. Safe bottling. Remember to
look both ways when you cross the harbour and
always wear your life jacket, even in bed, and
always keep a harpoon at the ready in case of
burglars.*

Signed,

The Message in a Bottle Lottery Manager

Mr Arthur Spooks

Tom did not spend too long admiring this message,
as he still had one more to do, and he hadn't even
started his homework yet. When the three messages
were all written and bottled, he would still somehow
have to make an excuse to get out of the house and
catch the tide.

Most people wanted to catch the post when they

35

had a letter to send. But Tom needed to catch the current. Still, if he missed it today, he could always get it tomorrow. Tides and postmen had a lot in common – they came and went with dependable regularity, and they kept on coming and going. But postmen got Christmas off, whereas the tide kept flowing no matter what, and it never took a holiday.

There was a knock on Tom's door. Without waiting for a response, his sister, Marie, stuck her head round the door.

'Did I say you could come in?' Tom asked her.

'Did you say I couldn't?' she said.

'What do you want?' he snapped.

'Mum says dinner will be ready in fifteen minutes and can you lay the table?'

'Why should I lay the table? What are *you* doing?'

'I'll be doing the washing-up. And she said have you done your homework yet?'

'What does it look like I'm doing?'

'Messing about with stupid bottles by the look of it. What are you doing? Opening your own bottle bank?'

'All right, I've got your message, thanks. Fifteen minutes.'

'What *are* you doing with those bottles, Tom?'

'What are you doing with your head round my door asking stupid questions, Marie?'

36

'Come on . . . can't you tell me?' Marie said.

'No, because you'll take the mick.'

'No, I won't.'

'You usually do.'

'I do not.'

'Then I'm writing messages, if you want to know, and putting them in bottles. And I'm sending them out to sea.'

Marie looked at him and screwed up her face. 'And who's going to read them then?'

'Whoever finds them.'

'And who's going to find them? Most of the world is water. Probably no one'll ever find them at all.'

'Somebody might. How do you know? It's bread on the waters. That's what it's called. Casting your bread on the waters.'

'Oh, bread on the waters – so you're feeding the seagulls as well then, are you?'

'See – I said you'd be stupid.'

'Not as stupid as you!' Marie told him.

'Well, you were born before I was, so you were stupid first,' Tom pointed out. He felt both hurt and offended. He knew he should never have told her anything.

'And then I grew up and learned not to be stupid,' Marie was saying. 'But it doesn't look like you ever will.'

37

Before Tom could think of a suitable riposte, she had closed the door and flounced off. Yes, that was just what she had done. She had flounced. Definitely.

It was irritating having an elder sister. Tom wondered if all elder sisters were so exasperating. He doubted it. Some of his friends' sisters seemed quite pleasant. Maybe it was only ever your own siblings who seemed stupid.

Tom took up his pen again.

Dear Stupid,

I see that you have been stupid enough to fish this mouldy old bottle out of the sea and to go to all the trouble of bringing it to dry land – or hauling it up on deck or whatever – and now you have opened it and are reading the message that was inside.

Well, I have to tell you that of all the stupid things you could have done, this is probably the stupidest.

Why on earth (or on sea) you think that you're going to get any sense at all out of a stupid old bottle, I do not know.

You would have to be stupid to imagine for one second that people who put messages in bottles and throw the bottles into the sea are sensible types. On the contrary, they are completely stupid. At least they are if you believe what people's sisters say, but personally I think all they talk is rubbish.

Yes, the chances of messages in bottles being found are so slim that only a stupid idiot would think it worthwhile sending them. And the chances of ever getting a reply are even thinner. So to hope for an answer is to be stupid beyond belief – according to sisters.

However, now that we have established how stupid you are for reading this message and how stupid I am for sending it, then maybe we can write to each other on a regular message-in-a-bottle basis and be friends.

It is my belief that we stupid types should stick together, because if we don't, then the cleverer sorts will come and get us. But I also think that as we outnumber the clever ones, then we have strength in numbers and so we will prevail.

Please send a stupid message back as soon as possible. It doesn't really matter what you write as long as it's something stupid. The chances are that I'll never get it anyway, so there's not much to lose.

Just for your information, I would like you to know that I am not the only stupid person in my house. I am really only an amateur stupid, but my sister is a professional. One day she hopes to get *paid for being stupid and to go on a TV talent show where her stupidity will be spotted and recognised internationally.*

We also have a cat in the house here who is so stupid he thinks he is a canary.

If you send a message back, don't forget to put the stopper back in the bottle, because if you don't, the water will get in and the bottle will sink. And that would be stupid.

However, even if you are stupid like me, please don't worry about it. For, if it is any consolation, no matter how stupid you are, there is always somebody in the world who is more stupid still – and her name is Marie Pellow. Thought you might like to know.

Yours sincerely,
The King of The Stupids, Arbuthnot Shanks,
The Idiot House
Dumbo Close
Thick as a Plank Walk
Stupidshire
Dunceville
STU P1D

Tom had just finished rolling this message up and sealing it into the old ginger-beer bottle when he heard his mother shouting up the stairs.

40

'Tom! I thought you were asked to come down and lay the table for dinner!'

'Coming,' he called back. 'Coming!'

He hurriedly put the bottles back upon the window sill, and clattered down the stairs.

He'd have to throw the bottles into the sea tomorrow. Too late to do it today. Maybe he'd be able to catch the morning tide. He'd check the tide tables. There was one pinned up on the cork board in the kitchen, along with the old postcards that people on holidays had sent them, and the scribbled telephone numbers, and the shopping lists, and the reminders of things to do.

Everyone in the village kept a tide table at home, somewhere handy. It was just what you did when you lived by the sea. Some people kept bus timetables on view. Others the times of trains. It just depended on what was important to you – on what you had to catch. And sailors and fishermen had to catch the tide. Miss it, and you'd be late. Miss it, and you'd be in trouble.

5

BAD BOTTLE WEATHER

The bay was visible from Tom's bedroom window, and on drawing the curtains the next morning he looked out to view the weather conditions. The tide was just turning, from slack water to outgoing, but there was not enough breeze there to even ruffle its surface.

Bad bottle weather, he decided. No sense in throwing his three messages out into the sea that morning. They wouldn't go anywhere. They'd just hang around like marker buoys, or wet leaves.

Tom put the bottles inside his wardrobe and covered them with clothes. That would do for now. He didn't like the idea of his mother reading them, but they wouldn't be there for long. He'd liberate them later, and set them loose on the evening tide.

After breakfast Tom made his way to school. Marie didn't have to go in that morning. She had exams coming up and was 'studying' at home. She'd better stay out of his room, that was all, and not stick her nosy conk into his bottles.

Tom's mother didn't go to work. That is, she worked, but she didn't need to travel to get there. She was a potter and worked from home. She made mugs and bowls and plates and jugs and cups and . . . well . . . *pots*, as a potter would. The kiln was at the rear of their house, attached to a small shop and gallery that had a note in the window saying 'Please Ring for Attention'.

In the summer the bell rang often; in the autumn and spring, not so much; in the winter, it hardly rang at all. But that didn't necessarily matter, for she also had a website and a *'presence on the internet'* as she rather grandly liked to describe it. So she also sold pots and ceramics by mail order and had what is known as a *'growing reputation as an artist'*. The storeroom round the back of the gallery was full of bubble wrap and Jiffy bags.

Tourists were their life-blood really. Since Tom's father had been lost at sea, the family was reliant on his mother's income. There were just two ways to make a living in the village – tourism and the fishing industry.

As a result the village and its surroundings were a contrast of hard practicalities and superfluous entertainments. There were trawlers, fishing boats, the cannery and the fish market. But then there were also tea shops and pasty shops; the places that sold knick-knacks and sketches of boats at harbour and puffins perched on cliffs. There was a surf school and a diving academy – at least in high season. The rest of the year the surf instructors did other things – painting and decorating, a bit of building work, stuff like that.

In the summer months the village was busy and it was hard to find anywhere to leave your car. Tourists wandered round, drinking everything in with their eyes, walking the heights of the coastal paths, then stopping off for cream teas. Or they relaxed in the sunshine and baked on the beaches. They lay on their towels and listened to the surf whispering, and they thought, *I could live here. Then I would have the sea and the sun and the sand and the surf every day.*

Of course, it wasn't quite like that. In the winter storms smashed the shore and men were lost. Trawlers went out but they did not always return. Men like Tom's father, who could not make a decent living at home, were obliged to travel to distant seas. It was common enough. You took the knowledge and skills you possessed and sold them wherever you could.

There were merchant seaman dotted all around the world who were Delwick men, born and bred. They stood on the decks and bridges of great liners and cargo ships – just like those presently moored at haven by the *King Billy* ferry. They could read a chart, navigate a course and manage a ship with the best of them.

But even the best and most skilful might not come

home one day. The sea did not discriminate. The careful and the careless, the ignorant and the knowledgeable, the cautious, the foolhardy, the prudent and imprudent alike – the sea could take them all if it wanted to. And no man's character and no man's skill was enough to defeat it.

Every sailor of any sense knew from the start that he was in an unequal contest, and that every time he got back to port, it wasn't ability alone that had taken him there, there was luck too. Luck and the weather. No wonder sailors were superstitious, even the most hard-headed of them. A lucky charm on a key ring, maybe; a St Christopher medallion on a chain a loved one had given. Don't get on board left leg first. Never drink all the tea from your tin mug, but chuck some over the side as an offering to the sea.

Like it would make any difference. Of course it wouldn't. And everyone knew it. And went on doing it, and always would. Some things were beyond logic, but you never knew, did you? Prevention was better than cure.

Tom had to catch a bus to get to school. The village was too small to sustain a school of its own. One was shared with half a dozen other villages, equally pictur-esque and equally small. As he waited at the stop by the harbour side for the bus to come, he watched the familiar scenes of men unloading boats, mending nets, tinkering with engines. There was the smell of fish and of seaweed in the air. All the activity and clutter seemed curiously timeless, like some ancient ritual, repeated daily and destined to go on for ever.

Some fishermen nodded to him and said hello and he nodded and said hello back. They didn't refer to his father any more. It was over a year now since he had been lost at sea. Tom wasn't the only one either, not by any means. There was probably not a single family in the village which had not, over the generations, lost someone in that way.

It was the farness though, Tom sometimes thought, the sheer distance. That was the hard thing. That his father should have been lost so far away, on the other side of the world. It was hard that there should be this great gulf, not merely that distance between the living and the dead, but the distance between the mourner and the mourned. There was nowhere to visit, no memorial, nowhere to go.

Sometimes Tom wondered if maybe, when the ship had gone down, his father had had a chance to write a message. Had he grabbed a pen, seized a scrap of paper, snatched a bottle as it rolled by and shaken the dregs from it, and put all three things to desperate, last-minute use? Was there a letter coming, even now, on its way, on the currents and the tides, on the Gulf Stream, maybe, heading in this direction?

What would he have written? What did you say when your ship went down with all hands – and that was what they had been told, all hands, the ship owners had said, all hands. No survivors, not one. Had there been a few moments, just a few, to scribble something, to say I love you or remember me? Or was the sea too cold around you? Were your hands too numb to hold a pencil and your fingers without feeling, and wrinkled white?

Beep, beep.

The school bus driver blasted his horn.

'You getting on or aren't you?'

The bus had been standing there in front of him for several seconds and the driver was a notoriously impatient man.

'What happened? Daydreaming again? I don't know, you kids, heads in the clouds.'

Though it wasn't the clouds. Not really. Tom had been at sea, far away. His head was in the foam and the spray.

He showed his bus pass and got on board. The bus continued along the coastal road, stopping to pick up more passengers. Tom nodded to a few friends and sat with them, finding a seat by the window. He pressed his head against the glass and watched the sea. The wind was picking up out there now. The waves had white caps to them and there was a visible swell in the channel.

A sailboat was out, alone in the coastal waters, white sails filling with the rising wind.

Tom thought of his mother. She'd be sitting down at the potter's wheel, her fingers wet and dirty with clay. The kiln would be firing up and the heat rising. Under her hands the first pot of the day would be taking shape. Other pots would be drying on the rack, and waiting to be decorated or glazed. She'd shown him how to do it, and he had tried, but he didn't have her knack. His pots just looked peculiar and his mugs had wonky bottoms and handles all askew. You'd have spilt your tea.

He'd take the three bottles up to Needle Rock later, he decided, and throw them as far from land as he could – so far that he wouldn't hear the splash, though he'd see it.

Yes, cast your bread upon the waters. And your hopes and dreams too. Then see what tomorrow might bring. Something good, perhaps, or something bad, or even a little of both.

There was something vital and real about it all though, he thought, something wild. Your message had to be tough to survive. It had to get through swirling whirl-pools and past sharp rocks and steer its way out to the shipping lanes and float on across deep and dangerous waters until it found the person fate intended it for.

Someone, somewhere.

Someone, somewhere would find one of the bottles. And they didn't even know it yet. But they would. Yes, they would.

Even now somebody might have found the first message he had sent out, two weeks ago now. Someone might be reaching for it, at this very moment, their fingers grasping for it, their mind thinking, *What's that? There's something in there! What is it? What could it be?*

Tom shifted in his seat. His stomach tingled with a vague anticipation, an excitement.

'Hey, Tom!'

Tom turned his head. Matt Coles was looking at him from between the seats.

'What?'

'What's so interesting out the window then?' Matt said. 'Spotted some pixies, have you?'

'No. But I've just spotted an idiot,' Tom said.

'That's funny,' Matt said. 'I'm looking at one myself.'

They grinned at each other – sharing insults was really a sign of friendship. Tom looked back at the view. Matt returned to his smartphone. Five minutes later the bus pulled up outside the school. But the day there seemed to take a long time to pass.

After dinner that evening Tom said he was going out for a walk, which earned him a few curious looks. He wasn't exactly famous for evening strolls.

'Well, all right, but be careful, Tom . . .'

'Mum! You don't have to tell me . . .'

She knew she didn't. But she told him anyway. She always would. The sea was an inescapable presence; it was there at the doorstep, all calm and smiles one minute, and snarling waves the next – a hand reaching out to take you.

Tom hid the three bottles under his coat, and left the house. He walked along by the harbour wall, and then headed up the coast path to Needle Rock. There was a towering pillar of granite there, called the Smokestack. From there Tom looked out at the horizon. The sun was stupendous that evening. It was like a blood orange, all reds and golds and yellows, like it was bursting open and bleeding over the sky and the sea.

Tom hurled the bottles far out into the water.

'There you go, and another one! That's three more for you!'

The tide took them, pouncing on them like some hungry animal, anxious to snatch its quarry and drag it back to its lair.

Tom's shoulder ached from throwing. He gently massaged his arm as he watched the bottles float out to sea.

Soon he had lost sight of them. The light was going now too. He turned back for home. A dog walker passed him on the way and said good evening.

By the time Tom got to his front door, the red of

the horizon was turning black. A last glimmer of light went from the sky, as if someone had closed a door. He saw the flashing lights from the marker buoys, out beyond the harbour, and heard the clanking of their bells.

Maybe he'd get a reply soon, he thought – an answer to one of his messages. There had to be someone out there, someone who was watching, waiting, listening. He couldn't be the only one, could he, looking for answers to float in on the rising tide and for deep-buried secrets to bob to the surface and sail in to shore?

Or maybe a message from his dad *was* coming, a bottle of words, a bottle of final, farewell words.

Because you wouldn't go without saying goodbye, would you? You couldn't go without saying good-bye. You'd want people to know, wouldn't you? That you'd thought of them, right up to the very end. You'd cast your thoughts upon the waters, even if it was the very last thing you did. Time and tide would take them and – even if it was a long, long journey – would one day bring them home.

Bottles had wings; like migrating birds they travelled long, lonely miles, vast distances, buffeted by wind and weather. Yet somehow – *somehow* – they always did find their way home.

6

MERMAIDS

More long days went by. In wanting to be reasonable, Tom grew unreasonable, and in trying to be patient, became ever less so. In telling himself that he should expect nothing, he constantly expected something – the glimpse of a bottle bobbing in the water, an answer, a reply.

At the weekends he might join his friends, surfing. But even as they paddled out in search of waves to ride back to the beach, he kept an eye out for the flash of green glass in the white foam.

He told himself it was ridiculous to feel this way, yet that was how he felt, and every evening, when the school bus dropped him off, he would make his way to the harbour before heading for home, and would stare out at the sea. And someone had noticed.

'Living in hopes, Tom?' Stovey asked him on one such evening.

Tom looked around to see the fisherman standing behind him. Stovey was old. He'd been a trawlerman all his life and had lost two fingers to the on-deck machinery. The winch had taken them. Yet he claimed he'd been lucky. 'What's a couple of fingers,' he always said, 'when others lose their lives?'

Tom didn't immediately answer Stovey's question. He guessed it was true, that he was living in hopes, but he didn't want to admit it. It was a bit of a sad thing to be living in hopes, because every unfulfilled day was another day of disappointment. And that was really a private matter.

'Hopes for what?' Tom replied cagily.

'I don't know, boy. You tell me. But I see you down at the water here every afternoon, looking out to the horizon like you are expecting to see your ship coming home. And a ship full of treasure at that.'

'No, not really, Stovey. I'm just looking. So what are you doing to your boat?' Tom asked him, to change the subject. 'Painting it?'

Stovey nodded, resigned and stoical, like a man without choices.

'You've always got to be at them, boats,' he said. 'Or they'll rot away and fall apart before your eyes and under your nose.' He stretched his aching shoulders and arms. 'With boats it's one day's sailing and one day's maintaining. Tedious, but it's got to be done. What do you think of her?'

Boats were always *hers* and *shes* to Stovey. He was

53

old school – very old school. More like ancient school, in fact.

'It's nice,' Tom said, admiring the shiny blue gloss paint. 'Looks like a different boat.'

'She does, doesn't she?' Stovey said. 'Amazing what a couple of licks with a brush can do. That's what you call refurbishment. Of course, the licks of paint are easy. It's the rubbing down previous with the sand-paper's the hard part.'

Tom was only half listening. His eyes were on the sea.

'What you looking for then?' Stovey said, following his gaze. 'Seals? Dolphins? A porpoise, maybe? You sure it's not your ship coming home?'

Tom felt himself blush. He would have liked to have told someone about the messages and his hopes of a reply. But some things, he felt instinctively, were better kept to yourself. What was serious to you could just be a joke for others. Look at Marie – for her it was all mere entertainment.

'I'm not really looking for anything,' Tom said. 'Just, you know . . . looking.'

'Then you shouldn't,' Stovey said. 'Not for too long.'

Tom glanced to see if he was joking, but Stovey's face was poker straight.

'Why not?' Tom said. 'What's the harm in looking out to sea?'

'It draws you in, that's what,' Stovey said with all

54

seriousness. 'The sea does. You look at it too long and too deep, you'll never get away from it.'

'Is that what happened to you then?' Tom said.

Stovey grinned at him with a smile so full of wrinkles he could have been made of them.

'Maybe,' he said. 'I never did get away, that's true enough. In fact, the sea's more home to me than dry land. And what's a boat anyway, if it's not a house on water? It's a floating bungalow, that cruiser of mine.'

Stovey kept a couple of rods and lines on board his small cabin cruiser, along with some crab pots and floats. He held a passenger licence, and in the busy season he might take fishermen out: holidaymakers and businessmen, in smart new waders, who made him look scruffier than ever. When the holiday season was over, he went fishing alone and sought out mackerel and lobsters for company. He also owned a row boat and a dinghy with an outboard. He had boats coming out of his ears.

Stovey was authentic in his way, the real thing, the genuine salt and barnacles. His features were tanned leather and weather-beaten. His shoulders were broad. His mane of thinning hair was white and straggly. His hands were gnarled, with swollen joints and scarred knuckles. He'd been a trawlerman since he was a teenage boy. Now he was in his sixties and still alive, just missing a couple of fingers was all. You could say he deserved to take things easy now, but easy wasn't how he liked it. The simple fact was that he preferred things tough.

Stovey had survived all the sea had thrown at him. But he wasn't triumphant in any way. He knew himself lucky. He gave the sea its due. He knew its strength. The sea could take anyone it chose to whenever it wanted.

'What *are* you looking for, boy?' he asked again, his curiosity still itching him.

'Nothing,' Tom assured him.

'You sure? You're staring out there like someone waiting for the postman to bring him his birthday cards or some cash from his Aunt Matilda.'

'No,' Tom said, a little disconcerted at Stovey's observation. 'I just like . . . looking.'

'I'll leave you to all your looking then,' Stovey said. 'But as I say, don't look too long and lingering, or it'll be after you.'

'What will?'

'What do you think? The sea will. Or the mermaids'll come and get you.'

'Don't be daft, Stovey, I'm too old to believe in mermaids.'

'Suit yourself. But I'll tell you this – it isn't whether you believe in mermaids that matters, it's whether they believe in you.'

'I bet you've never seen one though.'

56

'I have too. I've had them in the net. Caught them in the net and thrown them back in, as I didn't want them to get harmed, or to end up round the fishmonger's on a big, cold slab.'

'No, you didn't.'

He was such a liar, Stovey. He really was. But shameless with it, and convincing too.

'Might have done. One of them spoke to me. She said, "Thanks, Stovey, that's a favour I owe you. You call me when you're next in trouble". Said her name was Lucy, and she lived out by the breakwater.'

'You're just making that up, Stovey.'

'You think what you want, boy, but I wouldn't be so sure. There's more things in heaven and earth and on land and sea than any of us knows. I've even seen St Elmo's Fire with my own eyes. And the Northern Lights.'

'What's St Elmo's Fire?'

'You look it up on your internet. But when you see it, you'll think it's ghosts. And I've seen schools of dolphins swimming so close they looked like the curves of some great sea serpent. All sorts, I've seen. People didn't believe that fish could fly once. But I've seen them. Seen them hopping out of the water and flying after the boat. Seen the gulls snatching them in their beaks out of the very air.'

'That's different.'

'Is it though? You've not seen a mermaid, you say,

so they can't exist. Well, there's wider experience than your own.'

Tom shielded his eyes and looked out to sea.

'What's that?' he said. 'Can you see something there, floating in the water? Coming in on the tide?'

Stovey looked.

'Looks like an old milk crate to me,' he said.

'Ah,' Tom said, disappointed. 'Yes, I think you're right . . .'

'Or is it . . .' Stovey said, 'is it . . . some one-eyed monster of the deep, maybe?'

Tom could see the object more clearly now.

'No,' he said. 'It's a milk crate. It's a one-eyed milk crate of the deep.'

'The sea's turning into a rubbish dump,' Stovey said. 'When I started off, it was clean as tap water. Now it's all bags and trash.'

'If it comes in close enough to reach, I'll fish it out and put it in the rubbish skip,' Tom said.

'Good lad,' Stovey told him.

Stovey went to gather up his paint things and tools. It was time to go home. He did actually have a house, which he occasionally went back to; it was a tiny cottage at the top of the hill, with a small iron dolphin for a door knocker. It was time for him to put the kettle on now and drink some tea and then maybe close his eyes for half an hour, until he was ready to visit the Anchor Inn.

'I'll see you around then, lad,' Stovey said. 'Hope your ship comes home soon.'

'I'm not looking for anything,' Tom insisted. 'I'm not expecting anything. I'm just watching, that's all.'

Stovey packed up and left and Tom remained staring out towards the horizon. He wondered if he might see a bottle, slowly making its way towards him, a bottle with a letter inside for him, a bottle with a message and a meaning, a bottle with news in it and with things to say.

He went on looking until the light began to fade.

7

SALVAGE RIGHTS

Four bottles posted in total: three joke messages and one serious, but still, as yet, no replies. A whole month or more had already gone by. It was somewhat disappointing. Yet who, other than Tom, knew or cared? It was often the way somehow – what mattered to you the most meant little or nothing to others.

Tom wondered if he should try a few more messages and bottles. Or would that be like throwing good money after bad? Pity he wasn't able to track them – a little radio transponder in each bottle maybe, broadcasting its co-ordinates. Then he'd know just where each one was, and where it was headed.

Surely those bottles had to be out in the major shipping lanes by now. That was where the ocean currents and prevailing winds would have taken them – wouldn't they?

Tom asked Stovey about it one afternoon. He came across him down at the harbour again, covered in grease and overalls as usual, and looking for an excuse to take a break from his labours and have a spot of conversation. As ever, Stovey was working on his boat. Since he had given up the trawlers, there appeared to be an awful lot of tinkering about with the boats in his life, but not a great deal of actually going anywhere.

'Stovey . . .'

'What?'

'I've got a question . . .'

'Have you? Well, don't bank on anyone having an answer.'

'It's about the tide.'

Stovey raised one eyebrow in a question mark.

'What about it?'

'Just say something was thrown into the water, from Needle Rock, say, and then left to drift out on the sea. Where would the tide take it?'

Stovey looked at him, wondering where this was leading.

'What sort of something?'

Tom was reluctant to specify.

'Oh, you know, just something . . .'

'A floating something, or a sinking something?'

'Well, a floating something, obviously, or it would go straight down to the bottom.'

'You know that much then?'

'Of course I do.'

61

'Well, it's a start.'

There was another, longer pause, but no forthcoming explanation.

'So?' Tom prompted.

'So what?'

'Where would it go?'

'This floating something that somehow got chucked in the sea?'

'Yes.'

'Is it a big floating something or a small floating something?' Stovey asked.

'Small.'

'How small?'

'Just, you know, small.'

'Small-small? Or just small?'

'I don't know, Stovey, just small. I don't know how small small-small is supposed to be. But not big, that's all.' Tom was getting exasperated. Maybe he should never have started this.

'Well, is it as big as a rowing boat?'

'No.'

'Is it as big as a barrel?'

'No, smaller than that.'

'Heavy?'

'No, not heavy. I mean, light enough to float, obviously.'

'It's like twenty questions this game, boy.'

'What's that?'

'Haven't you played it?'

'No.'

'Well, never mind. Have you ever had a game of getting blood from stones?'

'Eh? What's that?'

'It's what we're doing, Tom, mate. Getting information out of you is like getting blood from stones – see.'

'I was only asking.'

'All right. And you're good at asking but not so hot on answering. Now what kind of thing in the sea are we talking about?'

Tom still didn't want to tell him. He didn't want to tell anyone and he wasn't going to. A secret is a secret, and a promise is a promise, even when it is one made only to yourself. He didn't want anybody else to know about the bottles. They were private, not public, matters – low-key and confidential.

'You know, Stovey, something light and small and buoyant.'

'Like a lifebelt maybe?'

'Sort of thing.'

Stovey narrowed his eyes, which glittered as he narrowed them. A sly look of understanding came over his face. It was actually a look of misunderstanding, but he was too pleased with his own canniness to imagine that he had got things wrong.

'I know what's up,' he said. 'I know what this is all about.'

Tom felt dismayed. People were always doing this. How come they could see into him, even when he tried his best to disguise his intentions? Was he that clear, that transparent? Could he never have secrets?

'What have you lost then, Tom? What have you lost?'

'Eh?'

'You've dropped something in the sea, haven't you, and you're wondering if the tide'll bring it back. What did you lose? Your surfboard or something? You forgot the tie around your ankle, did you, eh? Or did it just break off?'

'No.'

'Don't want to tell your mother, eh?'

'No, it's not . . .'

Stovey was tapping his nose with a gnarled and oily finger.

'Don't worry, boy, I won't say nothing. Your secret's safe with me.'

'I haven't got a secret,' Tom protested, which was untrue, because he had a bottle secret – but that, of course, wasn't the secret Stovey was talking about. It was annoying somehow when people accused you of harbouring secrets – when they were the wrong ones.

'Well, let me think then . . .'

Stovey ran his fingers through his straggly white hair, smoothing it down only for the breeze to ruffle it up again. Sometimes, in a strong wind, he looked like a cockatiel. He reached into his overalls, took out a beanie hat, and stuck it on his head.

'Okay . . . well . . .' He stared out beyond the harbour. 'You've got a chance of it coming back. It's hard to say. If it gets out a mile or two and hits the main current, you can say goodbye to it. It'll be off across the Atlantic then and you'll be lucky to see it again. But it might not get that far, see. There's a lot of swirls and cross currents out there, and the tide might well just bring it back in to land.'

'How long might that take?' Tom asked.

'Hard to say again. But if it hasn't come back in a couple of weeks, then you've likely had it. Unless it's already been carried back in, of course, and drifted up the haven.'

Tom stared at him.

'The haven?'

'Yeah. Rose Haven. Up by the *King Billy* ferry, where the big ships . . .'

'I know where it is, Stovey. My uncle captains the ferry.'

A disdainful look crossed Stovey's face, coupled with mild condescension.

'I don't know as being in charge of a back-and-forth

contraption that only ever goes one of two ways is what you'd call being a captain. I'd class it as more along the lines of bus driving. It's all "Fares, please," and "Hold on tightly, now," that kind of work. But you might go and have a look for your lost item up there.'

'But that's about two miles inland,' Tom said. 'How would anything get up there?'

'Doesn't make no difference,' Stovey told him. 'It's tidal. Things are always washing up in there. They won't always go out to sea. They might be carried back in, get stuck in one of the creeks. If you've lost your surfboard, boy, I'd go looking for it there. First port of call, I'd say. But if it ain't there and if more'n a couple of weeks are gone by, you've had it. Better buy a new one, Tom. Or keep an eye out for someone else's board getting washed up, and have that. Yours by rights, if you find it first and get it out the water.'

Stovey was right about that. Sometimes lost surf-boards did turn up on the beach and in the estuary.

'You can keep it too and all legal,' he said again. 'Laws of salvage, see. Finders keepers.'

Tom wasn't so sure about Stovey's interpretation of the salvage rules. What about that shipping container that had washed up on the beach a couple of years ago, full of tins of beans? The police had said taking the beans was stealing. No mention of salvage back

66

then. Not that anyone paid any attention. Nobody had stepped forward to claim them anyway. It was almost as if they were embarrassed to have so many beans in their possession.

'Yes, I'd go and have a look up Rose Haven, if I were you, Tom,' Stovey said.

'Would you?'

'I would. If it ain't there, then I think you can safely assume the sea's taken it and it's on its way to America by now.'

'America?' Tom felt impressed. Now that would be something – one of his bottles in New York City, or even gone to California.

'Or Africa maybe,' Stovey speculated.

'Africa? Really? So you think that if you threw . . .'

'Threw?'

'I mean lost . . .'

'Ah, right, lost . . .'

'If you lost . . . something in the sea, and it got out into the shipping lanes, it could end up in Africa?'

'Could do,' Stovey said. 'Easy.'

Tom wondered if, even at this very moment, some African fisherman had spotted a bottle bobbing about on the incoming tide, and he was leaving his nets, and running through the shallows and along the shore. And he was taking the bottle from the water, and removing the stopper, and extracting the message, and

67

reading the words: *Dear Finder, My name is Tom and I live in a place called Delwick, which is a small fishing village by the sea.*

Now that would be something indeed. That most definitely would be something. The man would take the bottle home and show the message to his family, and they'd compose a reply; they'd want to write back, of course they would. Once written, the new message would be put into the old bottle, and the stopper replaced. Then tomorrow the fisherman would return to the shore and throw the bottle out into the sea, so the outgoing tide could take it. Soon it would be on its way back.

Dear Tom, it would say. *My name is Michael and I am a fisherman in Africa. I found your message and showed it to my children who wanted me to write back to you . . .*

'Stovey . . .'

'You still here? You'd gone so quiet I thought you'd left.'

'I was thinking.'

'Oh, is that what it's called? I thought its name was daydreaming.'

'Stovey, how long would it take?'

'What take?'

'To get to Africa?'

'By what particular means of transportation?'

'You know, drifting on the tide.'

68

'Couple of months, I'd reckon. Why? You hoping someone'll find your surfboard and post it back? Got your name and address on it, have you? And a sticker saying "Return to Sender"?'

Tom wondered if Stovey had already figured out that he was really asking about bottles, not surfboards. Had Stovey ever sent off a message in a bottle? He might have. Even Stovey had been young once – many years ago, no doubt; centuries ago, even.

'No, I was just wondering,' Tom said. He felt a little dismayed. A couple of months for the bottle to get anywhere. That was a long time.

'Just say, Stovey, that something got to Africa on the tide, how long would it be before it came back?'

'More months,' Stovey said. 'If it ever got back at all. Months, years. It might have to circumnavigate the world.'

'What?'

'Go all the way around it. Don't they teach you what circumnavigation means at school?'

'I think I was away that day.'

'I bet. Away or fast asleep or looking out the window.'

'So realistically, Stovey, if you, well, dropped something into the sea here, and the tide took it, and it carried it out into the main currents in the ocean, and it went all around the world, it could take a whole year to go there and to come back?'

'If it came back at all.'

'That's a long time to wait, isn't it?' Tom said, dismayed. 'A long, long time. I mean, I'll be . . . I'll have had another birthday by then. I mean, next year, that's years away!'

Tom looked out at the sea. It was grey today and drab.

'I don't know if I can wait that long,' he said.

'Tom, boy,' Stovey said. 'Something you've got to know here – especially if you're planning on taking to the sea when you grow up.'

'My mum doesn't want that,' Tom said.

'No,' Stovey said. 'Neither did mine. But what you've got to learn, boy,' Stovey continued, 'is patience. You can't tell the sea what to do. It tells you. So you accommodate it. Nice and polite, like. You'll find, when it comes to the sea, that it's best to let it do the talking.'

Tom nodded, but it was only to keep Stovey happy. He'd rather have shaken his head than nodded it. It might have been the truth that Stovey spoke, but that didn't mean that Tom had to agree with it.

'I might go down to the haven, this weekend then,' he said.

'I would,' Stovey told him. 'Nothing to lose. Might find your surfboard there, languishing in the reeds. Unless one of those sailors has pinched it.'

'What sailors?'

'On the two big ships parked up there.'

'They wouldn't do that, would they?'

'It would be well within their rights. I've furnished half my house with salvage, boy, believe me. You can make a good living on what other people lose or throw away.'

'I'll go down on Saturday maybe,' Tom said.

'Well, I've got to get on now,' Stovey said. 'With a bit of work here.'

'Okay. Thanks then,' Tom said. 'I'll see you.'

'See you, boy,' Stovey said, and he watched as Tom turned his back and walked away.

He's a weird one, Stovey thought. And up to something too, no doubt.

Tom walked on up to Needle Rock and looked out over the grey sea. No bottles, no messages, no reply.

He would though, he'd go down to the haven at the weekend and say hello to Uncle Gareth and see if one of his bottles was floating around down there. Maybe a reply had already come. Things might travel faster than Stovey thought. Maybe the sea had a sense of urgency sometimes, and it gave special things priority.

Or maybe Tom's bottles and messages were in the belly of a whale somewhere. Like Jonah, in the Bible, who was swallowed whole. The whale spat him out eventually and it might do the same with the bottles. Only when? That was the question. How much longer would he have to wait?

8

MESSAGE FIVE – FINAL WARNING

Tom intended to get over to Rose Haven that weekend, but he didn't make it. His mother intervened.

'I need you to look after the shop,' she said. 'I'll be out all of Saturday and Sunday, on a course.'

A pottery course that was. She didn't take them, she gave them, at a local arts centre. The courses ran all day – lunch and afternoon tea included. She was well paid for it. But, at the same time, she didn't want to miss out on any sales from her studio. The weekends were always a good time. Even in winter there were usually a few visitors about, looking for presents and souvenirs.

'Why can't Marie do it?'

'Because she's playing the cello.' Marie belonged to the school orchestra. 'They've got rehearsals, all afternoon.'

'But I was thinking of going to see Uncle Gareth, and helping out on the ferry again.'

'Then you'll have to go next weekend, Tom. I'm sure he'll manage.'

'Ah but . . .'

It didn't do any good though. None of his 'ah buts' ever did. His mother always brushed them off as irrelevant. She had ah buts of her own, and they seemed to trump Tom's every time. It was like scissors, paper and stone, and she always had the winning hand.

'I'll be back by six,' she said. 'Seven at the latest. Keep the studio open until half past five or so. You can close it earlier if it's quiet.'

'All right then,' Tom said. He minded, but not that much. He quite liked being on his own and running the place – taking the money, wrapping the goods up, swathing them in bubble wrap to make sure they'd survive the journey, talking to the customers, who, he felt, were impressed by his age and efficiency, by the fact that one so young could be left in charge and given such responsibility. He could operate the card machine, and he always remembered to drop one of his mother's business cards into the bag, along with the receipt: *Dolphin Pottery and Ceramics, Delwick. Alison Fahler, prop.*, followed by her phone number and website address.

'Prop.' meant proprietor. Her name was Fahler because that was her maiden name. Pellow had been Tom's dad's name. His mum had kept her own, at least for professional purposes.

Being stuck in the shop all day on Saturday meant that Tom couldn't do much bottle spotting, which was a shame, because there was a bottle in the water that day, borne in to shore on the incoming tide.

Had Tom been down on the beach, or even up on Needle Rock with his binoculars, he might have seen it first. But as things were, he didn't – as he was soon to find out.

It was a fine day that Saturday. The shop and studio were usually warm anyway, due to the heat of the kiln. Tom opened the windows and sat back on his chair behind the till, waiting for customers. He'd brought his homework along, to fill the time. If he got it out of the way before the shop closed, he could spend the evening in front of the TV. His mother couldn't complain about that. Not if the homework was finished and he'd been working all day too.

In many ways Tom liked working in the shop, especially when he made a few sales. His mother's eyes always lit up when he told her about them. He felt he had contributed to the family finances then. He'd actually made some money. Sometimes Marie acted as though he was just a liability and an expense. Why did people do that? All because you were the youngest. Why did they heap it on you, like you were to blame for something? And just because you were last in line.

He'd been going to have a go at her about it once. He found her on her own in the living room and it seemed like a good moment. She hadn't seen him come in. But then he realised that she was sitting poring over the old photo albums, looking at pictures of when they had all been together, and there they were, Tom and Marie and Dad and Mum. And he realised that she was crying, so he turned and sneaked away again, and he never said anything.

Sometimes when people were nasty to you, they really meant something else. It wasn't really about you at all.

There was a steady stream of visitors to the studio that day. By two in the afternoon Tom had sold three vases, two mugs, a decorative plate and two solid ceramic cats which doubled up as bookends.

By three-thirty he'd done all his homework.

He went to have a look in the back, where his mother shaped and baked her pots, and where she kept the failures and the rejects. There was a bell on the shop/studio door, so if anyone came in while Tom was out of sight, he'd still hear them.

Tom peered around, examining the botched pots and the mugs that had gone askew.

It was odd, he thought, that his mother should be so skilled and adept at what she did, yet she went on having her failures. Not a lot of them, true. But she still had them, all the same. Did you ever get so good at something that nothing ever went wrong at all? He guessed not.

Trrring!

The shop bell tinkled. Tom stuck his head around the door.

'Hello.'

'Can we have a look around?'

'Please do. I'll just be in here.'

It was a couple with a dog. Fortunately they had left it outside, tied up to the park-your-dog-here post. You didn't want a St Bernard in a shop full of fragile pots.

As Tom looked at the rejects, one caught his eye. It was a vase. There were several in the shop – tall, elegant, bottle-shaped objects, designed to take one single, solitary flower; a tulip, or a lonely rose. This one had gone askew. It didn't sit straight, but leaned at an angle on its blistered base.

He picked it up. Ideal for a message at sea, he thought. Maybe he'd borrow that. His mother would never miss it; it was a reject anyway.

'Thank you!' The browsing customers called to him from the shop as they left. No sale this time. But they might return later. You never knew.

'Thank you,' Tom called back, poking his head round the door again in time to see the couple leave.

Right.

He sat at the desk and looked out of the window for inspiration. But it was hard to spot. Why did you always look out of the window for inspiration? Maybe you should look at your shoes instead.

He tapped his pen against the desk, then pulled the exercise pad over.

Hello . . . he wrote.

Nah.

He started on another page.

Hi . . .

Bit better. But not much.

If you like this bottle and want to order another one, or if you want to say hello, just email us at the address on the card.

He folded up one of his mother's Dolphin Pottery and Ceramics business cards and pushed it down into the bottle.

You might like to know that you probably have more chance of seeing a flying pig than of finding this bottle. So, if you have found it, then you must be a lucky person and you might even win the lottery as well.

Write back soon, if you can. I'm not throwing any more bottles out into the sea after this one, as I've already done several and had no replies. So this is my last one, and I hope it will be lucky, as

my mum made it, so it has got the personal touch.
     Yours,
     Tom

He rolled the paper up into a tube and poked it down inside the bottle alongside the business card. He rummaged around the studio until he found something to use as a stopper – a rubber plug, which he found in the back room. He didn't know what it had come off, but it would do.

At five-fifteen – having had no customers for the past half-hour – Tom decided that it would be okay to close early. So he locked up, took the bottle, and went down to the harbour. Stovey was working on his boat, across on the other side of the wall. He didn't see Tom, and Tom made no effort to attract his attention.

The tide was still on its way out, so Tom hurried up the coastal path to Needle Rock.

He checked that the stopper was tight in the neck of the bottle vase, then he made a few tentative, warm-up swings, and he flung the bottle for all he was worth, out into the sea.

He saw the splash, but didn't hear it, for the swirl of the water on the crags below drowned it out.

The tide took the bottle and carried it away. It seemed like a bottle of some intelligence and sense, for it skilfully avoided the rocks that would have smashed it to pieces, and it bypassed the small whirlpools which would have sucked it down.

In minutes it was on its way, out to open sea. Tom watched it go, then looked at the time on his watch. He wanted to be back before his mother returned.

'That's the last one though,' he said out loud. 'If I don't get any answers this time,' he shouted to the sea, 'then I'm not writing to you any more. You understand? This is your last chance. Your very last chance. Or I'm finished with you. You won't get me too. You owe me an apology, see. You need to say you're sorry, for all you've done and all the misery you've caused.'

He raised his fist in defiance. He didn't shake it. Just raised it, so the sea could understand that he really meant business this time.

But the sea just plunged on, in its aimless, shapeless way, with its eternal, mindless indifference to all human affairs, to all mortal losses and gains, and to all human feeling. It didn't need you or require your approval or forgiveness. It just was. It didn't care who sailed on it, or who didn't; who survived or who drowned; who lived, who died. Nothing mattered, not to the sea. It just was.

'I've warned you!' Tom cried. 'That's your last one!'

He turned for home. The seagulls were squawking on the cliffs above. They had no interest in him either. Every living creature in the world seemed entirely absorbed in itself.

9

ANY OTHER BUSINESS

It turned out that somebody else had discovered what Tom had been looking and hoping for – a bottle in the sea, swept in on the tide. The finder was another pupil at his school.

When Tom heard news of this, what rankled with him was the sheer unfairness of it. R.D. hadn't even been searching for bottles. He'd just been poking around on Tolzeth beach, hunting for lost coins and loose change and pebbles of unusual sizes.

And there was the bottle, lying on the wet sand, abandoned by the high water, which had retreated and left it behind, along with a few plastic bags and some driftwood.

Everyone called Richard Davenford 'R.D.' – to such an extent that some people didn't actually know his real name. He was a bit weird – but harmless. Tom had never had reason to dislike him before, but he felt some resentment now.

R.D. was in Tom's class, or Tom was in his, depending on how you saw it. R.D. sat at the back with a nice daydreaming view out of the window, which he frequently put to good use.

It was the Monday after Tom had looked after the pottery shop. During the noon lesson, shortly before lunch, the teacher had introduced a new ten-minute spot called Any Other Business. It was basically Show and Tell under another name, but as they were all too old for that, she called it A.O.B. to make it sound more interesting and sophisticated.

Anybody could take part in Any Other Business – you just needed to stick your hand up. You didn't necessarily have to bring something along with you to show. Any Other Business could be a complaint, an observation, an appeal, an exposure of some perceived injustice. Someone had even got up once and sang a song – to general hilarity and some groans.

R.D. wasted no time in putting his hand up when Any Other Business was called, and he was invited to stand and to reveal what his Any Other Business was.

He extracted an object from his backpack and held it up.

'I found this,' he said. 'On the beach on Sunday.'

'What is it, R.D?' some wit called out – for it was blatantly obvious what the thing was.

'It's a bottle,' R.D. said.

'Get away!' the wit replied. 'Never!'

The trouble was that although R.D. was not exactly

slow on the uptake, he wasn't quick on it either. He was . . . well . . . individual. And it certainly wasn't that he was stupid. He was more . . . well . . . gullible: a willing believer in conspiracy theories who possibly watched too much sci-fi on the television.

'This bottle,' R.D. went on gravely, 'is no ordinary bottle.'

'Is it a special bottle then, R.D?' the wit – May Clarke – asked.

'Quiet, May, please,' their teacher said.

'It *is* a special bottle,' R.D. confirmed. 'Now, you may wonder why–'

'Is it made out of diamonds?' May asked.

'May, I'm warning you,' the teacher said.

'This bottle is special,' R.D. said, 'because it has a message in it. A message for us all.'

'Ooooh!' May said. 'Just fancy!' But she didn't really sound that impressed.

Tom sat up at news of this discovery. He felt hurt and angry. Why had R.D. been permitted to find such a bottle – when Tom had been the one waiting for a reply? When he had been the one sending all those messages out to the sea. And now that an answer had finally come, it had gone to the wrong address. R.D. had got his paws on it. And what did it say? It had to be a message intended for Tom. R.D. had picked up Tom's mail by mistake.

'This message that I found . . . this important message . . .'

'Get on with it, R.D. . . .'

'Yeah, get on with it.'

'Stop spinning it out, will ya?'

The class was losing interest. Many of the individual pupils had long attention spans, but the collective one was short.

'Yes, if we could hurry things along a little, Richard,' the teacher said. 'It will be lunchtime soon.'

As soon as that bell went the room would be empty. You wouldn't get people hanging round to hear what messages in bottles had to say, not once the canteen was open.

'This is the message here,' R.D. said. 'Just as I found it.'

He stuck the narrowest of his chubby fingers into the bottle and prised the rolled-up message out from the neck.

'I'll read you what it says. I think it's quite important too. I think it's something that we need to tell the whole world. For it is a message for all us earthlings – from another planet.'

R.D. said this with no trace of irony in his voice and with no expression of humour on his face. He believed what he was saying. But before he read a word out, Tom already knew what was coming. And no wonder. After all, he had written it.

'Dear Bottle Finder,' R.D. read out. Then, just to clarify, he explained to the rest of the class that: 'That means me, as I found the bottle.'

'Get on with it, R.D., or I'll be asleep soon.'

'You won't fall asleep when you hear this,' R.D. said. 'The message continues: I am an alien being from another planet, and I wish to communicate with you earthlings. I come in peace. I have dropped this bottle into your ocean from a great height, from miles up in space, where I wait in my spaceship, along with plenty of food and a big flat-screen TV.'

'Come on, R.D. – sit down, will you. Give it a rest.'

'You wrote that yourself, did you?'

'I did not,' R.D. said indignantly. 'I found this on the beach, just like I said. It's a message for planet earth from an advanced alien intelligence, warning us all of the error of our ways.'

A ball of paper winged through the air from the back of the class and struck R.D. on the head. He didn't seem to notice. The paper just bounced off.

'Don't do that, whoever threw it.'

Miss Reverton picked the paper ball up and binned it.

'Quickly now, please, R.D, if you must,' she said, looking at her watch.

'It's important, miss,' R.D. said.

'Well, just hurry it along.'

R.D. licked his lips and read on.

'. . . This bottle,' he read, holding it up for all to see, 'is made of a special glass, unknown to earthlings, and it can withstand great temperatures, which is why it did not melt as it fell through your atmosphere, and is why it did not break when it landed in the water, even though it is like hitting concrete when you fall from a great height.'

'Don't be stupid. It's an old cola bottle.'

'It's from Zark of the Alien Brotherhood, as a matter of fact,' R.D. said angrily. 'And people like you ought to listen. The message goes on to say: "I would appear in person to you, only my appearance would be so frightening to you that you would probably wet your trousers if you ever saw me."'

'I wet my trousers first time I clapped eyes on you, R.D.'

'That's enough,' Miss Reverton said. 'Quite enough.' She was starting to feel a sense of losing control. R.D. and his message in a bottle had not been a good idea. She might suspend Any Other Business for a couple of weeks to give it a rest. It was getting stale.

'The note goes on to say, and this is very, very important,' R.D. careered unstoppably on, his voice rising, his hand tapping the desk for emphasis. 'It says: "we wish to make contact with you, to warn you that you need to sort yourselves out a bit. You need to do something about global warming and all the litter on the beach. As aliens of superior intelligence, we also have to tell you that you give your school children far too much homework to do and as a result you are burning their brains out and giving them mental breakdowns . . ."'

There was an uproar of laughter, which, fortunately for everyone – and especially for Miss Reverton – coincided with the ringing of the bell for the end of the lesson.

'All right, leave quietly, please, in an orderly manner. Thank you, Richard. I'm sorry we don't have any more time, but that was very interesting.'

'But, miss, there's a message here from the aliens, for all humanity . . . this is important, miss . . .'

'Yes, all right, thank you, Richard. But you run along now and have your lunch. Thank you for bringing it in. Don't forget there is a maths assessment this afternoon, so be back promptly – that's everyone. Okay?'

'But, miss – the message, miss, in the bottle . . .'

It was no good. Half the class had gone, and the rest were on their way.

Tom didn't feel so bad now that he knew R.D. had only gone and found one of his bottles. It was a little worrying though, because that meant that the bottle hadn't really gone anywhere. It had just been carried out to sea and then brought back in. It had ended up at almost the same place as it had started. Tolzeth beach was only about half a mile from where Tom had thrown the bottle in.

But R.D. was visibly upset. Miss Reverton looked at him with sympathy, but with some impatience too.

'Richard,' she said, 'I think someone was having a joke, that's all. Why don't you go and have your lunch?'

R.D. looked from her to the message to the bottle and back to the message again. Should he keep it or should he tear it up?

He decided to keep it. He rolled it up, poked it down into the bottle, then returned the precious bottle to his backpack. Maybe one day, perhaps years from now, the prophecies the note contained would come true. Then people would know that it really had been a message from aliens, and it genuinely had been a special alien bottle. It maybe looked like an ordinary cola bottle, true enough, but that was just the cleverness of it. If the glass was ever analysed, it would be of a type unknown to mankind. R.D. was sure of that.

R.D. made his way to the canteen. Everyone seemed to have forgotten all about his Any Other Business and his message in the bottle. As he stood in the queue, he realised that Tom Pellow was staring at him. Maybe Tom was interested, R.D. thought. Maybe Tom might like R.D. to join him at his table in a minute, and they could talk aliens, and messages, and special bottles, and of Zark of the Alien Brotherhood.

But when their eyes met, Tom immediately looked away, and he struck up a conversation with somebody else.

10

REPLY

The following weekend, Tom had time to himself. It was his sister Marie's turn to help out with the shop, so there was no reason for him to stay at the house. He told his mother that he was going up to the river estuary, to help Uncle Gareth on the ferry. But his real motive was to search for bottles.

Tom was worried that maybe Stovey was right in his calculations, and that the tide would wash the bottles he had thrown back to land and into Rose Haven itself. If one had turned up at Tolzeth beach, and R.D. had found it, it seemed all too possible.

By the same token, any replies to his messages might end up in Rose Haven too.

So he got his bike out of the shed and set off on the road to the ferry. It was across at the other side of the estuary when he got there, loading up with cars and passengers. It was a strange thing, Tom thought, that no matter how many people were queuing up to head off in one direction, there were always other people wanting to go the opposite way. People never seemed to be satisfied with where they were, and just yearned to be somewhere else.

As he waited for the ferry to come back over, some cars and foot-passengers arrived on his side. The ferry wasn't a fast mover; it chugged along back and forth at little more than walking pace. Gareth saw him waiting as the ferry slowly pulled in, and gave him a cursory nod. He wasn't the most demonstrative of men, Tom's uncle. But just because he didn't smile much, it didn't mean he wasn't pleased to see you.

'All right, Tom?'

'I thought I might come down and see if you needed any help.'

'We're all right, but you can come along for the ride – such as it is.'

'I can collect a few fares if you like.'

'Okay then, but keep out of the way until the cars are on.'

He didn't need to say so. Tom knew what to do and where to stand and how not to be a nuisance.

The cars drove on board and the foot-passengers followed; there were a couple of cyclists too, with panniers all over their bicycles.

The windlass chains rattled as the ramp was raised. The siren blasted, and the ferry chugged away again on its relentless journey: back and forth, there and here, for ever and ever, amen – crossing that same few

90

hundred metres of water until its engines gave out or its hull rusted away or until its skipper finally had a mental breakdown and decided to jump into the water in an effort to end it all, as he had had enough.

Yet Uncle Gareth appeared as indifferent as ever to the tedium and repetition of his life.

'A job's a job,' he'd often say, as if to imply that any other work would be no more interesting. 'At least it's steady,' he'd say.

Too steady, Tom thought.

He stowed his bike in the Staff Only cabin and went to help collect the fares. He said hello to Mike, the regular crewman, whose job it was to wave the motorists on and off and to make sure they paid.

Tom also got a satchel and a wad of tickets. They were all in different colours, green for Foot Passengers, blue for Motorists, purple for Vans, brown for Lorries and Buses, yellow for Motorbikes, white for Bicycles, and they came in Singles or Returns.

As the ferry pulled into mid-river, Tom looked upstream. He saw the two huge cargo ships at anchor, still moored in Rose Haven. This close, they were simply colossal – almost unimaginably so. Nothing for miles around was as big as those ships. Not a hotel, not a mansion, not a sports centre, not even the local hospital was as big as one of those vessels. They would have dwarfed the town hall and the church. The small village cinema would have fitted into one of the holds quite easily, with plenty of room left over.

'When are they going, Uncle Gareth?' Tom asked. 'They've been there a long time.'

He shrugged.

'They'll go when they're needed,' he said. 'When the cargo business gets busy again and the economy picks up. Cheaper to have them parked up here than gulping diesel down, sailing round half empty and rattling about the oceans.'

Tom watched as they passed by the ships. On one of them a cradle dangled from a winch on the upper deck. Two men were on it, suspended precariously, at work on the hull. They were mid-way between the top of the boat and the waterline. If the cradle ropes snapped, they'd have a long fall down.

'What are they doing?' Tom asked.

'Maintenance,' Gareth said. 'Always stuff to do on boats.'

'That's what Stovey says too,' Tom told him.

Tom saw that the two men on the cradle were rubbing down the hull with blocks and sandpaper. Red dust floated away on the breeze – rust flakes and old paint.

'What a job,' Tom said. 'I mean, how long would it take you to paint the whole hull like that?'

'Months, probably,' Gareth said. 'Years, even. I don't know how they can stand a job like that. I couldn't abide the tedium, myself.'

Tom looked at his uncle, but didn't say anything.

Anyway, maybe those two sailors were quite happy working away and having something to do. Maybe they even enjoyed the endless rubbing down and painting, though Tom couldn't really see how. But then Gareth appeared to like what he did – or at least he didn't seem to dislike it.

I couldn't do that, Tom thought. Never. Paint a whole ship, one that size.

He had a different, more interesting future planned. Maybe he could get taken on, on one of the Delwick trawlers, and get his seaman's papers. That would be the life. A hard life, but never dull. His mother wouldn't like it, of course. She wanted him to keep his feet on solid earth. She'd put glue on the soles of his shoes, if she could, to anchor him for ever to dry land. It was part of the reason why Tom sometimes felt he had to slip away, to escape from his mother's worry and from his irritatingly sensible sister, and to crew with Gareth or listen to old Stovey spinning fanciful yarns out of fishing nets and crab pots. The sea was in all his stories; they were full of rock pools and smelt of brine.

Tom kept watching the men on the cradle, curious.

They were very different in stature, though hard to make out in detail. Against the bulk of the ship they looked tiny and ant-like. One man was small, thin and wiry, and his skin was brown – he looked as if he came from somewhere far away, Malaysia or Indo-China: Vietnam, perhaps, or Cambodia.

The other man on the cradle towered over him. He could have been a Westerner. But he was very tanned and his hair was so long and unkempt that it was turning into dreadlocks. It was truly hard to tell what he looked like at that distance. He could have been almost any nationality. As for his face, it was so swathed in a thick, dark beard that he seemed to be mostly whiskers.

As the ferry moved on towards the opposite bank, the bend in the river caused the two big cargo ships to disappear from view. The ships vanished from sight – still there, but no longer visible. It was like that game you played when you were small, with the flat of your hand in front of your face – now you see me, now you don't.

Back and forth, back and forth the ferry ran. Refreshments on the move; hot chocolate at eleven; lunch at one. As they went, Tom kept scanning the water for a glimpse of shimmering glass. Surely he had to see a bottle, sooner or later. Everything comes to those who wait. And he had waited – quite long enough. So it was time now for something to come to him. What were fate and chance doing sending bottles to people who didn't understand or properly appreciate them? People like R.D., who was just ridiculous and believed in aliens.

'What you looking for, Tom?' Gareth asked him. 'You lost something?'

'No, no,' Tom said. 'Just, you know . . . looking.'

'Want a rod?' Gareth offered.

'All right. Yes, I will. Thanks.'

'Keep it out the way, mind. Don't go snagging any passengers with the hook.'

Gareth kept a couple of fishing rods and a few lines on board, and he sometimes draped and dangled them over the side of the ferry, to see if fish might take the bait as they chugged along. Mostly, they didn't, but sometimes they did. He didn't always use fresh bait, sometimes just metal spinners attached to the lines, bright silver in colour, dashing through the water, trying to trick the bigger fish into believing they were sprats. Then the big fish would swim up, open their mouths, clamp their jaws shut and . . .

'Hey, Tom, boy. Looks like you've got one!'

Tom wound the line in. The fish floundered on the deck, the barb of the hook in the flesh of its mouth. It wasn't such a big fish, not worth keeping, Tom was relieved to see.

'Too small, Tom. Just chuck him back.'

Tom liked catching, but not keeping them. He didn't like to see the fish die, lying there breathless. It was a kind of drowning, only in reverse – the fish squirming there, panting for water.

He held the too-small fish in one hand and carefully extracted the hook from its mouth with the other. Then he flipped the fish back over the side into the water, and it swam off to live a little longer and grow a little bigger, and – who knew – maybe be caught again.

And that was when Tom saw it. Just as he was about to cast the line out. He saw it, there in the water, bobbing along, close to the downstream side of the ferry and drawing nearer. There it was at last! A bottle. It was a bottle. A sealed bottle, with its stopper in place. There was something inside it too, there really was. A message. An answer had finally come.

'Gareth . . .'

'Hold on, boy. We're docking in a minute.'

Gareth might have docked the boat several thousand times before, but he still needed to concentrate.

He got the boat in, and Mike secured the ropes. The ramp was lowered and the cars drove off.

'Gareth . . .'

'What's up? You off home?'

'No. But have you got a net?'

96

'A net?'

'You know – a fishing net. On a pole. A long one?'

'What? A net for tiddlers? There should be one with the tackle in the cabin there. Why?'

'I saw something in the water.'

'What?'

'I think it's for me.'

'Tom, what are you on about?'

'There's a bottle out there.'

'Bottle of what?'

'No, it's just a bottle – a special bottle. I need to get it.'

'What you want a bottle for?'

'It just looks important.'

'Important? An important-looking bottle? What's an important-looking bottle look like when it's at home?'

It wasn't at home though, was it? It had gone travelling.

'There it is look, there.'

Tom pointed. The bottle was in mid-stream and drifting. In a few more minutes it would be out of reach.

'Can we go, Gareth? Can we go and get it?'

'Don't be daft, Tom. We've got to load the ferry.'

Tom went to the deck rail. Mike and Gareth waved the cars on. The bottle was drifting away, Tom saw. He felt anguished. He even thought of jumping in and

97

swimming to get it. But he knew that would be stupid. The water was deep here, and very cold. He could drown – and even if he didn't he'd have to face Gareth's wrath when they fished him out of the water.

Come on, come on, come on! willed Tom.

Why did they move so slowly? Why was everyone taking so long? Why had they all started to move in slow motion, as if wading through treacle, like men in dreams?

At last. A blast from the siren and the ferry pulled out. Gareth didn't say a word, but he steered the boat slightly off its usual course so that the port-side deck came near to where the bottle was still bobbing on the current.

Tom had the net ready. He saw some of the ferry passengers grinning at him, wondering what he was up to, amused by the frown of serious concentration on his face.

Well, stuff them. What did they know? He scooped with the net. He had it – almost. But when he went to lift the bottle out, it slipped away. And the ferry was moving ahead. One last chance. Tom stretched out, long and far, his arm at full reach.

'Careful, boy. What you doing?'

He felt someone hold him. Mike had grabbed his belt.

'You'll be in, in a minute, Tom, boy. What's up with you?'

'It's all right, Mike . . . I've got it.'

He had too. It was in the net now, and he drew it in, up on to the deck, careful not to drop it.

'Got it, see!'

Mike looked at him as if he were mad.

'It's just a flipping bottle, boy.'

But it didn't matter. It didn't matter that Mike could neither perceive, nor understand its significance. It was a bottle, yes, but not just any old bottle. It was *his* bottle; it was meant for him. And Tom could clearly see, as he took the bottle and untangled it from the net, that there really was something inside it, just as he had thought. A paper, neatly rolled and waiting to be unravelled. There was a message. There really was. There was a reply. There was an answer. There was a message in the bottle.

But when to read it? Where? Here? Now? No. Later. Somewhere private.

'So what're you going to do with that bottle then, Tom?' Mike said. 'Now you've near half killed yourself getting it out the water.'

'Oh, just keep it, you know.'

They hadn't noticed that there was anything inside it, and Tom wanted things to stay that way. If Mike and Gareth saw there was a message, they might want to read it too.

'It don't look that special, that bottle,' Gareth

99

observed. 'I thought it was going to be a real old one or something. You know – a collector's item.'

Tom wished he had something to hide the bottle in – a deep pocket, a carrier bag. Then he remembered his bike.

'I'll just go put it in the pannier. Make sure it doesn't get broken.'

He did, and then, when the *King Billy* ferry came back to Brent's Landing, Tom announced that he would head home.

'Good to see you then, Tom. Regards to your mum.'

'Thanks for having me on board.'

'Any time. Thanks for helping.'

'Bye, Mike.'

'See you, Tom.'

They watched as he wheeled his bike off.

'He's a bit of a deep one sometimes, isn't he?' Mike said when Tom was out of earshot.

Gareth looked towards his departing nephew with some sympathy and sadness. 'Well, you have to make allowances, Mike, I guess, after all that happened.'

'They never found anyone from that ship his dad was on?' Mike said. 'Not a soul?'

'No. Boat went down with all hands. They found some wreckage, but that was it. No survivors. Gave up looking in the end.'

The ferry crossed mid-river. The two great cargo

vessels again came into view, at anchor in the haven. The painters' cradle had been hoisted up. It was empty now and the men had gone.

'It was a ship the size of them, was it?' Mike said. 'Big merchant job?'

'Yes,' Gareth said. 'She rolled and went under. Storm in the Pacific. Force twelve gale. They reckon her cargo shifted.'

Yet, as they stood there at anchor in Rose Haven, the two huge ships appeared unsinkable. How could anything so mighty fall victim to the sea?

Gareth glanced over his shoulder to see his nephew still standing by the ferry station. He was peering into the bottle he had found, like someone gazing into a telescope. Then he replaced the bottle into the pannier of his bicycle and rode away.

Gareth turned his attention back to the wheel. You could even sink a back-and-forth ferry if you didn't watch what you were doing. The deep water just never let up on you. It was full of tricks like that.

11

ABLE SEAMAN BONES

As soon as he was half a mile from the *King Billy* ferry, and felt confident that he was no longer under observation, Tom stopped and rested his bike against a fence, and took the bottle from the pannier.

The bottle, Tom was convinced, was the same one. It was the bottle he had used for his very first message, the one that had begun: *Dear Finder, My name is Tom and I live in a place called Delwick, which is a small fishing village by the sea.*

It had been a screw-top, just like this one, and the same colour too, the same dark green glass – an old fizzy mineral water bottle, he was sure of it.

Wasn't he? Well, he was, sort of. Only now he looked at it more closely, he wasn't quite as sure as he had first thought. The glass was rougher and more scratched than he remembered. But its weeks at sea could account for that.

The other, more puzzling thing was that Tom had put his email address on the message. So, if someone had found it, why hadn't they emailed him? Why would they try to reply in a bottle when the chances of it ever being found by the sender of the first message were so impossibly slim as to be almost non-existent?

There was only one way to find out.

He held the bottle to the light. It was semi-opaque, but even so, he could see that what was inside was not his original letter. It didn't even look like paper that was rolled up in there. It was some other material: something softer and more pliant.

A car zoomed past. It had probably just come off the ferry. A couple of motorbikes went by too, then the road fell to silence. Tom wanted to open the bottle, yet not here. The place didn't feel right somehow, not secret enough. He'd get the bottle home first and lock the bedroom door behind him. Privacy, quiet – no Marie barging in uninvited. She could bang on the door all she liked, she wouldn't be getting in.

Yes. Home first. That would feel better. Get it home and up to his room, close the door, then sit down and slowly unscrew the cap, and take out the rolled-up message inside. Take his time, savour the moment . . .

But when he arrived back there were jobs and chores waiting for him – a trip to the village shop, a bag of logs to fetch, then there was dinner. It was another two hours before he was safely in his room.

He stood the bottle on top of his desk. The outside

of it was bone dry now; the glass was foggy with scratches and abrasion. It was a bottle that had travelled, there was no doubt about that. It was a bottle that had seen the world. A watery world, admittedly, but still a world further afield than Delwick.

A vaguely fishy odour of seaweed and brine rose from the bottle, as if despite its dryness, the sea had somehow got into its fabric, and would be there always.

Tom took the neck of the bottle in one hand and held the bottom of it in the other. He tried to unscrew the stopper, but it seemed jammed or rusted on. He got a cloth from the bathroom, and wrapped that around the bottle cap to get a better grip.

Finally the cap turned. He unscrewed it fully and removed it from the neck. He peered down. There was some kind of fabric in there, tightly rolled. Tom prodded it with the tip of his finger. It looked, it felt, like a piece of canvas. He tilted the bottle and tried to prise it out, but it wouldn't come.

He took a pencil from the drawer, upturned the bottle, and tried again. It took him a few goes, but he succeeded. Out the rolled-up material came. It was damp, as though water had got into the bottle during its journey, and the smell of the sea was quite pungent.

It dripped a few drops of water as Tom unravelled it, and the brine splashed on to the carpet. But Tom

104

was oblivious to it. For he saw, as he unrolled the piece of canvas, that there was thin and spidery writing upon it, as if written by some feeble, if not ghostly, hand.

Tom flattened the canvas. When spread out, it was maybe the size of two A4 sheets of paper. The writing was neat and ordered, but it had an old-fashioned look to it, for it was all in italics. It didn't seem to have been written with any ordinary pen. It looked as though the writer had used a quill, or a nib, or the thin, sharp end of a razor shell. For the message had been as much scratched into the canvas as written upon it. The ink was very faint and pale.

All the same, the message was legible. Tom smoothed the canvas carefully once more, to make sure that it lay flat, then he began to read.

Dear Shipmate, the words began,

I don't know if you'll ever be reading this, for the sea's a wide and wandering thing, and even the best of mariners can't always say for sure which way the tide will run. We know which way it ought to go, or which way it usually goes, but which way it will go is always another matter. The sea's an independent-minded sort of thing, that follows its own fancy.

105

But all the same, if we found your message, then there has to be a chance that you'll find ours. For that's how things go, in the give and take and the back and forth of fate and circumstance.

I'm just responding to say hello back to ye, and that it's good to hear from someone who ain't afeared to cast their bread upon the waters - someone who has faith in the fates and the prevailing winds and the drift of the sea. For without all that, there's no sailing, nor sailors either, and that's what we all are here - or were, at least.

So a big hello to ye, from all of us here. We call ourselves the Ancient Mariners, though some of us are no more than boys - or were when we first came here. It's down in Davy Jones's Locker we are - or, at least, that's as good a name for the place as any.

Some of us have been here a long time, while others have come but lately. There's always new members joining, though it's never - or rarely - by choice. But here we are, and here we stay, forgotten mostly. Most of us are so old there's no one left to remember us. But some still have loved ones out there, who remember them dearly and miss them much.

And it's sad they are from the thinking of it.

Prayers are never wasted, but it's memories that mean the most to an Ancient Mariner. It's knowing there's someone out there, on some patch of dry land, still thinking of ye and keeping ye in their hearts.

There's a saying that dead men tell no tales. But that's not the case. They do nothing else down here. Tales and fine-spun yarns and historicals going so far back you wonder the world could be so old and still have folk remembering it.

That's how it is in the Locker. Some folk go to eternal rest, but the likes of us - the seafaring men - we stay for ever. In our element, you might say, until the day the sea gives up its dead. Till it surrenders all those who once conducted their business in great waters, just like the Good Book says. And we've not so happy that we couldn't be happier, but we've not so sad neither. We have company and yarns and jellyfish passing and coral waving and turtles nodding hello on their way by.

So, good to hear from you, shipmate. And good luck in all that you do. If you ever choose the seafaring life, then always wear your life preserver on deck and never scoff at the safety drill and always know how to swim - though if that sea cold ever gets into your bones, swimming won't do much good, and that's Neptune's truth.

Good luck and good seafaring.

Regards on behalf of all down in the Locker and from all us Ancient Mariners, both young and old.

Yours,

Ted Bones (or so folks choose to call me, humorous-like. I was once an able seaman, back upon a while. But am no longer as able as I was. Write back, if you wish, as it's many a long year since we had a correspondence. What news? Are we still at war with the Frenchies? Or is all that over and done?)

P.S. What's an email address, shipmate, as you mention in your letter? I ain't heard of that in any of my travels.

Tom stared at the message. He picked the piece of canvas up and turned it over, in case there was more written on the back, and he had missed it. But no. He had read it all.

He sat, shocked. He looked around the room. It was on the tip of his tongue to call out, 'Mum! Marie! Come here and look at this!' He had feared their interference, but now suddenly he craved their company.

Yet something stopped him and held him back.

He read the message again, and as he did, an increasing coldness came over him.

'It's a letter from a dead man,' he whispered. 'It's a message from the dead.'

Tom had the sudden, frightening feeling, that there was someone at his shoulder, someone right there behind him, peering at the message, reading it alongside him.

He spun around.

'Hey!'

There was no one. Just him in the room, alone, and the faint sound of sea, which was always present, day and night, and the distant, intermittent warning siren of the marker buoy, far off, near Black Rocks.

His skin tingled. What did it mean? How could it be possible? How could it be a reply from some dead, drowned sailor, some old, ancient mariner, with a razor shell writing implement, and a scrap of torn canvas for his writing pad, and a squirt of squid ink for his pen?

That sort of thing was all just fantasy, wasn't it?

The stuff of pirate films. All that business about Davy Jones's Locker, down at the bottom of the sea, where dead sailors congregated, puffing on empty pipes and drinking from tankards which held only salt water. That was just a story. It wasn't real. When you drowned, it was the end of you. You didn't live on in some underwater garden, swapping yarns with other sailors, and watching the starfish tiptoe by.

And how would anyone at the bottom of the sea have found Tom's message? Unless the bottle had sunk somehow, or the ghostly soul had reached up from their briny tomb and snatched it from the waves.

Or was it a joke?

That was it. A joke. Someone had found the bottle and had decided to play a joke. It was R.D. getting his own back for the aliens.

And yet . . . it didn't feel like a joke. There was something about the spidery handwriting and the frayed canvas that seemed all too ancient and real.

Tom went to the window. He could just make out the marker buoy, as it blinked and gave off its warning light, regular as clockwork, every forty-five seconds.

The sea appeared calm tonight. The tide was running in gently, and you could hear the soft sound of undertow, of smooth grinding pebbles and shifting sand.

Was it really possible that lost souls were out there,

deep at the bottom of the sea? Where the hulks of stricken ships gradually turned to rust and barnacles, but with their crews still on board – rolling a set of ghostly dice, playing a hand of phantom cards, gurgling a sea shanty as the living passed above them on cargo boats and cruise liners and as trawlers spread out their nets?

Tom picked the message up. The canvas felt grainy yet delicate, as though it might easily flake away, and the writing upon it turn to dust. It was drying out in the heat of the room. Tom hurried to the bathroom and turned on the tap. If he didn't keep it moist, it would crumble away. And then what evidence, what proof would he have? Who would ever believe him then? Not that he was going to tell anyone about it. Not yet.

He re-rolled the message, and he returned it to the bottle, and replaced the cap. He hid the bottle in his wardrobe, well concealed under old, unused toys and unplayed games and forgotten jigsaws. He lay on his bed, with his hands behind his head, staring up at the ceiling. The ceiling light was not on, just the bedside one. He fell into a kind of trance, one of almost pure thought and little feeling. He had to decide what to do, how to react to this, how to respond.

I'll write back, he decided. I'll write back and see what happens. If they found my first message, then they'll find the next – won't they? Of course they will. It stands to reason.

Tom went on lying there on the bed, composing messages and letters in his mind, then dismissing them immediately as being inadequate and wrong. He'd get it right yet. He'd think of what to say.

Only what did you say to a dead man, down at the bottom of the ocean? What did you say to old Ted Bones and to all the Ancient Mariners?

He'd think of something though. He knew he would. Just give it time. Sleep on it, maybe. Then write down, and bottle up, his words and thoughts and send them off to the sea. For if old Ted Bones could find one bottle, then Ted Bones could find another. It stood to reason.

Yet a part of Tom's mind clearly understood that reason had nothing to do with it whatsoever. There was no reason in any of it at all.

12

DEAR MR BONES

Reply, reply. What should he write? Should he use the same bottle again? Or a different one? No, the same one, surely. If Ted Bones was looking out for an answer, then he'd be looking for the same container.

Frustrated, indecisive, Tom threw his pen across the room and fell back on to his bed. He felt as though his mind were squirming. Ridiculous. There was no Ted Bones. It was a stupid, made-up name. There were no Ancient Mariners. There was no Davy Jones's Locker either at the bottom of any sea. It was just stupid, and Tom knew it. Not stupid to send the first message, no. That had been fine – an experiment, a bit of fun. But this. This was stupid. When people drowned, they drowned. They were dead and they stayed dead. They couldn't even think a thought, never mind write one down.

Someone was having him on. But who? Who knew? Who knew that he had thrown a message in a bottle into the sea, apart from Marie? There was nobody.

Not a soul. And if anyone was playing a trick on him – and it wouldn't be her – then why had they waited so long? And what kind of a trick was it to play? They couldn't have known that he would find the bottle. So why would you bother to play a practical joke like that, when there was no certainty of it working? That wasn't much of a joke at all.

But if Tom were to write back now, that *would* be the joke – getting him to do so, making him look stupid enough to believe that there was a dead Ted Bones at the bottom of the sea who, despite the inconvenience of being deceased, still knew how to maintain a correspondence.

Oh, drat it.

He got up and retrieved the pen. He opened the door of his room and peered out. Light was coming from under Marie's door. Maybe he should go and talk to her? No. She'd just take the mickey and tell him he was stupid for even considering it. And he knew that already.

His mum? No. Not her either. It would upset her. It would bring thoughts of his dad back, and his being lost at sea, all those thousands of miles away, and never being found.

Who then? Was there anyone? Anyone at school? No. Not really. Plenty of people he could talk to about other things, but not this.

How about Uncle Gareth? No. He'd just say, 'Don't be daft, boy. Go out and do a bit of surfing, clear your head and get you thinking properly again.'

Then Tom thought of someone – Stovey. Old Stovey. He'd listen. He knew all about the sea and its superstitions. None of it would be new to him. He wouldn't tell you not to be stupid and snigger at you behind your back. But should Tom show him the actual message he had got from Ted Bones? Or just talk about it all in general terms?

Tom sat on his bed and picked up his writing pad. Right. He'd tell Stovey and get his advice, but not yet. He'd send off one reply first, and see where that led. If he wrote back to Ted Bones and nothing happened, then that was it all over and done with. If time went by and the bottle didn't return with a fresh message from Ted Bones inside – or if Tom never found it – then that was it. Forget about it. Just . . . let it all evaporate. Let the memories vanish, like mist and dew, drying in the morning sun.

He felt better now, calmer, more at ease. Things were all right once you had made a decision on what to do.

Okay then. So what to say to old Ted Bones, down there in his watery home?

Dear Ted . . .

No. Maybe not. Too informal.

Dear Mr Bones . . .

Yes. That was better. Nice and polite.

*Dear Mr Bones, Thank you for your message of
. . .*

Tom had been going to write the date of Ted Bones's letter. But the message was undated, he remembered. Well, it would be, when Tom thought about it. Nobody would be too bothered about the time or date, not down in Davy Jones's Locker.

Tom did a bit of scratching out, but no matter, this was just the rough copy. He'd re-write in full before putting it into the bottle.

Dear Mr Bones,

Thank you for your message in the bottle. It arrived just yesterday. I found it down at Rose Haven, where the great big ships are moored, as you might know. Or more likely things were different back when you were still sailing the seas. But Rose Haven is a safe harbour now and ships come to it from all round the world, as far away as China.

It was very kind of you to write back to me. It has been many weeks since I threw the bottle into the sea, and I had almost given up on it ever being found.

I must admit that I did not expect to get a

116

message back from an Ancient Mariner down in Davy Jones's Locker. It sounds to me – and please don't take this the wrong way – but it sounds to me as if you are a bit dead.

Is that correct? Are you all dead, down in Davy Jones's Locker? And, if so, how do you manage to write letters? And what do you do all day? And can you still feel things? And, if so, is it cold?

I see that in your P.S. you ask what an email address is. But I don't really think I can explain that very well, to be honest, as first you would have to know what a computer is, and I suspect, from some of the other things you said in your message, that you wouldn't know what that is either. But basically, it's a kind of mail box. But you need a computer to use one, and I don't imagine you'll have a computer at the bottom of the sea, as the electrics would get wet and then it wouldn't work – so you wouldn't be able to email me anyway.

You asked if we were still at war with the French and the answer is no. We've not been at war with France for years and years – since long, long before I was born. In fact we get on rather well with the French, most of the time, and a lot of people go there for their holidays.

117

Tom paused. He sucked the end of the pen. What else? What else could he say? Something important, something significant, something that might prove, one way or another, whether Ted Bones was a hoaxer or not.

What could Tom ask? How could he get old Ted Bones to betray himself as the practical joker he had to be?

The sucking turned to chewing. Tom worked the small blue stopper at the end of the biro out with his teeth, and then he began to munch away on it, as if it were a piece of gum.

Had to be something. Had to be.

He got it. It came to him so suddenly, so clearly, that he reacted physically to the arrival of the thought. He went cold, then felt his heart beating faster. Yes. He'd got it. Yes.

He spat the blue end of the biro out into his hand. It was so misshapen now it wouldn't go back into the pen tube. He flicked it into the bin.

I wonder if I could ask you something, Mr Bones, about your shipmates down in Davy Jones's Locker, for I guess that you must know them all. I know someone too, who was lost at sea, and not so long ago either. Just over a year, that's all. His name was – his name is – Samuel Pellow. Could you say hello to him for me? He isn't all that old, about the same age as my mum. He was a sailor, just like you. His boat was in a bad storm and the cargo shifted and the boat unbalanced and went down with all hands – and those hands were never found, even though other ships went looking for survivors. They looked for days and days, but in the end they called the search off. It all happened so swiftly and suddenly they said that no one would have had a chance.

Would you do that for me please, Mr Bones? I want him to know that we are all well here even though we miss him dreadfully and think of him every single day.

Will you say that, please, Mr Bones, and then write back with news?

Thank you.

I will sign off now and put this letter into the bottle – well, it's our bottle now, I suppose: yours and mine – and then I will go down to the harbour later and throw it into the sea for you to find. Which I hope you do.

Thanks for writing back to me.

A big hello to all down in Davy Jones's Locker.

Sincerely,

Your friend,

Tom

119

When he had copied it all out again and corrected the mistakes, Tom went to the wardrobe and took out the green bottle. The message on canvas, that Ted Bones had sent, he extracted, dampened with water and wrapped in a plastic bag which he then hid at the bottom of his chest of drawers, right at the very bottom, where no one would discover it.

He rolled up his newly written message, inserted it into the bottle, and tightly secured the cap.

With the bottle in the pocket of his coat, Tom quietly left the house. He didn't even tell anyone he was going out, for it was late now and dark – but he wanted to catch the tide.

The village streets were deserted and silent – except across the harbour, where lights were blazing in the Anchor Inn, and from which came sounds of laughter and of music.

The tide was soon about to turn. On impulse, Tom decided against the harbour, and headed again up the coastal path to Needle Rock. It only took ten minutes to clamber up there. Standing next to the Smokestack, he hurled the bottle into the black and foaming sea. It immediately disappeared. There wasn't enough light for him to see it by now or to track its progress seaward.

There. It was done now. The message was written and dispatched. Nothing to do but to wait again – to wait for old Ted Bones to get his squid ink and his scallop shell and a fresh sail remnant out and to start writing.

Or maybe Ted Bones didn't write things himself. Maybe he had an octopus that took dictation, and it wrote down all he said in its very best handwriting.

How strange, he thought as he looked out towards the sea, that he should have been born here in this village, and not in some land-locked place where people never ventured on to ships and never drowned.

But you couldn't choose where you were born. You couldn't choose many things about your life, really. You were at the mercy of fate and circumstance, and you bobbed around and went wherever the tides took you, like a small, helpless, directionless bottle in the immense and powerful sea.

And maybe you had a message inside you, or maybe not. If someone were to find you, what would you reveal? What news, what words of wisdom would you have for the world? What would people think of you if they could read every one of your secrets?

Tom watched the surf for a few moments more, then headed back down the hill. Soon he was home again, opening the door quietly, and tiptoeing in.

13

OCEAN PEARL

When anxiously expecting a letter, what was worse: fearing it might never come, or going on believing that it would, but plainly not today, for the tide had already been and gone, and delivered nothing?

Tomorrow then? Was that reasonable? Or too soon? How long should you expect to wait? Would a reply come with tomorrow's tide? Or never turn up at all? Worse still, would someone else find it? What then?

It was complicated, collecting your seaborne mail. This wasn't like running down the stairs first thing on Christmas Day, to see what presents had been piled up under the tree for you. Nor like clattering down those same stairs on the morning of your birthday, to see what the postman was pushing through the letter box – all those cards and packages and envelopes. Waiting for a message in a bottle was a far more uncertain business.

Tom felt like someone marooned on a desert island. He had cast his bread upon the salty waters. His cry for help was out there on the ocean. All he could do now was watch and wait, and keep hoping.

He went past the harbour every morning on his way to the bus stop, and on his return in the afternoon he scoured the beach. After tea and homework, he would stroll up to Needle Rock to survey the sea, or wander over to the sands of Tolzeth beach.

If the weather was right and the waves were good, he might join the clumps of surfers, looking vaguely like seals and penguins in their glistening neoprene. Occasionally he ran into R.D. from school, with his battered old surfboard and lumpy wetsuit, and would surf with him for a while. He wasn't that bad really, Tom thought, just awkward and clumsy, and maybe a bit lonely. Tom felt he knew about that too. Part of you was always lonely when you had lost your dad, and no amount of company could ever fill the void.

At weekends he cycled to the *King Billy* ferry, where Gareth was starting to wonder why he had become so frequent a visitor. Was he after a job? Did he want to be skipper of the ferry one day, like his uncle? But no, it was something else, Gareth decided. The boy was always half distracted, his mind never fully on his work. He was always scanning the waters, like he was hoping to find another of those bottles floating by. Small chance of that though.

Gareth had found a bottle himself once, back when

he was a boy. There'd been a message in it. He'd been delighted and had carried it home in triumph. He'd got his mother to open it for him and to tell him what was in there, as he was too young to read.

It had all been in Chinese. At least it had looked Chinese. It definitely wasn't English. Gareth had kept the message for years, hoping one day to get it translated. When it finally was, all it said was: *Good luck to you, bottle finder, and a big hello from Japan.* He'd felt a bit disappointed; he'd hoped for more.

Gareth still had the bottle though, in his living room, with a dried flower stuck in it. He'd never found another good bottle – not one with anything in it. Just plastic ones and bits of rubbish. So if it was rare bottles young Tom was after, he'd be lucky to find any, no matter how long and hard he looked. One good bottle was all you got in this life – that was Gareth's opinion. Most people found no bottles at all. Besides, you didn't want to be greedy. You couldn't expect more than your share.

The world is full of sayings: some of them wise, some of them foolish; some of them true, but not always.
Everything comes to those who wait.
Maybe. Sometimes.
It depends on what they're waiting for.
A week went by. Two. Two and a half, then two and three-quarters. Two and six-sevenths and finally

124

three. Three and a seventh and eventually four whole weeks had passed. Four whole weeks of waiting.

What was up with old Ted Bones? Why didn't he write back? Why didn't he respond? How many pen and bottle friends did he have? Had he other commitments? Did he spend his whole life – well, his death – at the bottom of the briny ocean, keeping up a correspondence with shipmates all around the world?

What if he hadn't got Tom's message?

No, surely he would. Even if the bottle had sunk, he would still get it. That was where Davy Jones's Locker was – down where all the sinking stuff settled, where it came to rest, where it could fall no further.

Tom brooded and obsessed. He grew so withdrawn and silent that his mother couldn't help but notice. He got tetchy, short-tempered. She talked to him about it in the kitchen one evening.

'What's got into you, Tom? Are you all right?'

'Nothing, Mum. I'm fine.'

'You don't seem able to sit still for even three minutes.'

'I'm just going down to the harbour.'

'Again? You were there this morning.'

'I like the harbour.'

'Why don't you go and see one of your friends? Go surfing maybe?'

'No, I'm not in the mood right now.'

125

Although maybe he should, after all. If he went out on his surfboard, he might find the bottle. He could meet it halfway.

He took up his mother's suggestion and went down to join the surfers. There was always someone down there that he knew. R.D. was there again, falling off his board as usual. But there wasn't a bottle anywhere in sight.

Tom spent an hour in the sea, but then – despite the wetsuit – he got cold. So cold he couldn't feel his feet any more. And his eyes stung from the salt. He came out of the water and went home.

'Good time, Tom?'

'Yes, fine, Mum, thanks.'

But still no message, no bottle, no reply.

On the following weekend, he joined Uncle Gareth again, for another Saturday's work on the ferry. The two big ships were still at anchor in Rose Haven – the *Ocean Emerald* and the *Ocean Pearl*; one emerald green, the other pearl grey.

'I think they must be sisters,' Gareth said, looking at the two hulks. And they probably were. They were identical, apart from their colours; they flew the same flags and bore the same owner's name and logo.

'Do they still have their captains on board?' Tom asked.

'No,' Gareth said. 'Just a junior navigating officer, maybe, and an engineer, and a couple of hands. You wouldn't want to pay a captain's salary for him to sit idle for weeks on end. Only a skeleton crew on each ship. They'll fly the captain back in when they need to get moving again.'

'Don't the crew ever get to come on shore?' Tom said. 'Seems tough to be left on board for so long.'

'They do and they don't,' Gareth said. 'That is, they used to get to come visiting. Until a load of them from the *Port Sally* that was moored here last August decided to go and get stuck into the beer at the Anchor Inn one night. The result was what you might call havoc. Shore leave's been a bit curtailed since that happened. I think this lot are all doing penance for the sins of others.'

The two men on the cradle were still there, still rubbing down and painting the hull of the *Ocean Pearl*.

'It's Little and Large, look!' Gareth said. 'You noticed the pair of them?'

Tom's eyes followed Gareth's pointing finger, but his mind was off elsewhere.

The smaller of the two toiling men – the thin, dark and wiry one – appeared to be in charge, the one making the decisions as to when to lower or raise the cradle, when to stop work and when to take a break.

The taller, lighter skinned man was more solidly built, and his unkempt hair and untrimmed beard hid him, as if he were in disguise. They both worked doggedly and patiently, rubbing down, cleaning off, applying fresh paint, moving on to the next section of the hull.

The smaller man seemed to treat his companion with some sympathy and concern, – which indeed was so – as if he were worried that his shipmate might wrong foot himself and plunge from the cradle into the water. And this was also the case.

The fact was that the smaller man, Keo, who was indeed Cambodian, had pulled his companion from the sea once already, and he didn't want to do it again. His companion, whom he called Charlie – not because that necessarily was his name, but because it was a Western name that Keo had heard a lot – had been lucky to survive his last tumble into the ocean. Nor had he emerged from it unscathed. The scar on his head attested to this. It was long and deep and had taken quite some time to heal.

Having pulled Charlie from the water once, Keo did not want to have to rescue him again. So it was best that he didn't fall in a second time. And to make sure he didn't, Keo kept a close eye on him. For it is a curious aspect of human nature that if you rescue someone from near death, you can become surprisingly fond of them. And having gone to all the trouble of once saving them, you don't want them dying on you now.

'You okay, Charlie?'

'Fine,' Charlie grunted. He didn't say much. Keo didn't either. He didn't know a lot of English and Charlie knew no Cambodian. But for all that, they rubbed along companionably enough. They just got on with their painting, and waited for the eventual command to come from the ship owners that a cargo had been found, and their ship was needed to carry it. Then they would up anchor and leave Rose Haven, heading out for open sea.

Off the ship would go into the vast, wide ocean, brushing flotsam and jetsam aside, as its propeller threshed the water and drove it on, leaving foam in its wake, with birds flying above the churned-up water, and with perhaps even a lost bottle or two, bobbing in the sea behind.

14

NEWS

Old Ted Bones
Old Ted Bones
Listen to how
His bones all groan
His ship went down
His shipmates moaned
And that was the end of
Old Ted Bones

The rhyme Tom had made up went compulsively around in his mind as he cycled home from the *King Billy* ferry late that Saturday afternoon. It went round his head the way his feet went round the pedals. When his feet sped up, the rhyme did too. When he slowed on an uphill, so did the verse. He couldn't make it stop.

Uncle Gareth had given him wages for his work on the ferry, so he had money lying itchy in his pocket. Mike had taken the afternoon off and Tom had collected all the fares on his own. He had been useful.

Instead of going straight home, he cycled to the harbour, and inspected the incoming tide. He wondered how he might spend his earnings, and his thoughts inevitably turned to the small village shop and to the bars of chocolate upon its counter.

He was just about to go there, before it closed. The sun was sinking, but its light suddenly hit something that shined and sparkled. Tom realised what it was at once. It was a bottle, drifting in with the rising water. And not just any bottle – *his* bottle, surely. It had to be – if there was any justice, or if wishing and longing could make it so.

Ted Bones must have written back.

Or maybe it was only Tom's own message returning to him.

There was but one way to find out.

The bottle was a good hundred and fifty metres away, maybe more. Tom looked around, wondering how he was going to get to it. Then he spotted Stovey, tinkering with a lobster pot on the harbour wall.

'Stovey! Stovey!' Tom hurried over. 'Can I borrow your dinghy for five minutes?'

Stovey looked at him with curiosity.

'What for?'

'I want to get that bottle.'

Tom pointed to it. Stovey looked out.

'I don't see no bottle.'

'There – *there*!' Tom said, but Stovey still couldn't see it.

'What you want that bottle for anyway?'

'I just do. Can I borrow your dinghy? Please. I won't go outside of the harbour.'

Stovey considered this.

'No,' he said. 'But, as a favour, I'll row you. Put that life jacket on first.'

Tom bristled.

'It's only a short distance. It's in the harbour. I can swim. It's not deep.'

'It's deep enough to drown in. Listen, boy,' Stovey said, 'if you think I'm taking you out in a boat anywhere without a life jacket on, you'm entirely wrong. Your mother would kill me – twice. So put it on, or we don't go.'

Tom put the life jacket on, though he noticed that Stovey didn't, not even for the sake of good example. Stovey didn't bother with the outboard motor either. It wasn't worth the trouble. He slotted the oars into the rowlocks and in a couple of minutes they were out by the bottle.

On the way, Stovey made a half-hearted attempt at conversation.

'How's your mum?' he asked. 'She managing?'

'She's all right,' Tom said.

132

'And how's your sister?'

'All right,' Tom said. Though whether she was or not, he didn't really know.

A few more strokes of the oars and they were beside the bottle. Tom reached over and fished it from the sea.

'Don't look specially old to me,' Stovey said. 'You collect them, do you?'

'Sort of,' Tom said. He swiftly put the bottle out of sight behind a coil of rope by his seat. He didn't want Stovey thinking or knowing there was a message in it. So quickly did he hide it, he didn't get a proper look at it himself. The dark green glass protected what was in there from easy view. Tom's curiosity would have to wait a little longer to be satisfied.

'That it?' Stovey said. 'All done?'

'Yes, thanks,' Tom said.

'No other bits of rubbish you want to take home with you? A few plastic bags? A bit of fishing line? A couple of cods' heads?'

'Just the bottle, thanks.'

'Okay.' Stovey turned the boat around. 'If I see any more like that one, I'll let you know.'

'Thanks,' Tom said.

They tied up at the harbour wall and clambered out of the dinghy.

'Want an old lobster pot, do you?' Stovey said.

'What for?' Tom asked.

133

'Ornament,' Stovey said. 'Look nice and nautical about the place. Keep it in your room, or use it for decoration in the shop.'

'Won't it smell fishy?'

'It'll wear off.'

'Don't know if my mum would like it.'

'I'll give it you anyway. You see what she says.'

'Thanks.'

Tom handed the life jacket back and Stovey threw it into the dinghy. He thanked Stovey once more, took the old lobster pot and headed home, pushing his bike along with the lobster pot dangling from the handle-bars and the bottle inside the pot.

When he got back, he left the lobster pot in the greenhouse and put his bike in the shed. His mother was working. He called hello.

'I'm just finishing something,' she said. 'I'll be in soon. Marie's not here for supper. She's going over to John's when she's finished her essay.'

Marie had a boyfriend now. She was having dinner at his house. They'd mooch about the harbour after, sitting on the bench and looking at the moon. Tom had seen them. They'd been holding hands. It just made you queasy.

He went up to his room. He set the bottle down upon the desk. He touched the sand-roughened, pitted glass.

It wasn't only messages that came in bottles, was it? he thought, as his fingers traced its surface. Genies came in bottles too. And when you removed the stopper to let them out – so the story went – you could never get them back in again. They created havoc and mischief in the world and you rued the day you'd ever set them free.

But he knew that he would still open it, whatever the consequences might be.

15

DEAR SHIPMATE

Most people look for refreshment in bottles – for water, wine, lemonade, beer. Sometimes it is medicine they're after – linctus or cough syrup. But you don't expect to open up a bottle and for a stream of words to pour out into your glass.

Back in his room, Tom unscrewed the cap. There was that familiar smell of the ocean. It was salty, musty, musky, fishy – an odour of nets and old timber, of mussels in rock pools and seaweed on the shore.

Inside was another piece of sail canvas, ragged-edged and frayed and tightly rolled. He upturned the bottle and shook it. A few drops of water fell on to the carpet. The rolled-up canvas protruded from the bottle neck. Tom pinched it between finger and thumb and tugged it out. It felt damp and cold. Some powdery crystals of salt were visible upon it. He brushed them away, like dust, then delicately unrolled the thin canvas, as if afraid that it might crack and disintegrate.

Where the message had come from, or how it had arrived, no longer concerned him. The impossibility of dead men putting pen to paper wasn't relevant. It didn't matter. In a universe full of mysteries and impossibilities, what was one more? He just wanted to read what was written here. What did this new message say?

Dear Shipmate,

Good to be hearing from you again. As you'll no doubt be knowing, bottle post ain't the most efficient means of lettering people. But it seems like it's all there is for us old sailors here, down in the Locker. We can't be sending no writings by mail coach or carrier pigeon or by messenger on a swift horse. Not even a seahorse, shipmate - as the letters would be bigger'n they are.

But no worry. Your reply fell into good hands. And it got to me eventual-wise, for a shipmate can trust a shipmate down here like he was his own brother - which he might even be - and a letter'll always get passed on. Just remember to write specific that it's for old Ted Bones.

So then. I'd imagine you've been growing impatient for news and maybe wondering when an answer was going to come.

Now, in your message that you wrote recent,

137

you made enquiries, I believe, as to a Mister Samuel Pellow - was the name you used. You didn't say exactly what the connection was, shipmate, but you seemed to speak of him affectionate-like, and you came across as sort of anxious that a good word of remembering should be passed on to him - which is the sort of good word that mariners greatly appreciate down here.

Well then, matey, when old Ted Bones is asked to pass a word on, then that's just what he does. He don't let no obstacles stand in his way when it comes to the execution of his duties and his social obligations.

But you'll understand, I'm sure, matey, that the Locker down here is a big, wide place, with many a mile of cavern and cave and wrecked ship and coral reef. It can take a time for the making of enquiries and the asking of questions and the passing on of messages from elsewhere such as the world above.

So that's another cause of delaying, see. It ain't 'cause old Ted Bones has been idle, it's more 'cause he's been working so hard.

I have to tell ye, matey - and don't take it wrong - but I have to tell ye that I've put out feelers like an octopus here, like a great long jellyfish with mile-long spreading tendrils. I've passed on word everywhere and I've listened out with an ear like a conch shell for the reply to come.

But for all my asking, matey, there ain't no answer come, for no one down here has any acquaintance with any Mister Samuel Pellow. Not in any familiar and present way. There's some that says they know his name, and there's some that says they were shipmates even, back upon a time. But there's none as says they've shipmates still and that he's down here in the Locker.

So what I'm saying to you, matey, is that either you have his name wrong or you don't have the facts right of the case. If there ain't no Sammy Pellow here, then he ain't been taken, shipmate, not by the sea. Either he's up there still with you, or the dry-land's got him, and he's resting easy in some old church yard somewhere-abouts. If so, I hope it's not too landward, but more with a coastal feel to it. For a sailor likes a view of the sea and to have his feet pointing in the right direction, even when he can't sail no more.

I'm sorry, shipmate, that I can't give you no more definite news. All I can say is that wherever this Mister Samuel Pellow is that you're looking for, he ain't down here with us in Davy Jones's Locker. So I hope you find him elsewhere-abouts.

You take care now, matey, and if there's anything else old Ted Bones can ever do for a shipmate, then you just ask away. For there ain't no harm in asking, especially if it's done polite - as it has been.

Good sailing to ye and fine weather always.
Your shipmate down in Davy Jones's Locker,
Ted Bones

Tom stood and closed the window vent. He went and felt the radiator with his hand. It was on and it was hot. So why did he feel so cold? So suddenly, terribly cold.

He blew on his hands, but it wasn't really them that the chill came from. It was inside him, in his chest, his core, in his heart.

So what I'm saying to you, matey, is that either you have his name wrong or you don't have the facts right of the case. If there ain't no Sammy Pellow here, then he ain't been taken, shipmate, not by the sea.

But that wasn't possible. He'd been gone over a year now. His boat had gone down, 'with all hands' – *all hands*. Not a single man was rescued, although they had looked for days and days. No one was ever found. No one.

Tom re-read the letter. He paced the room. What should he do? Whom should he tell? Shouldn't he tell his mother, at once, immediately, right now? Tell her the news, the unbelievable, fantastic, the glorious news . . . ?

No. He couldn't. Because that's just what it was – unbelievable. How could it be true?

Marie then? Could he confide in her? They didn't have much to do with each other, even though they lived in the same house. She was older and had her own friends and he was the younger brother she now had little time for. But she was still his sister.

Tom hesitated. Then he went to his drawer and found the first message. He picked up both pieces of canvas with the same scratchy, spidery writing upon them. He went out into the corridor and knocked on the door of her room. He could hear her inside. She hadn't yet left.

'Marie . . .'

'What do you want? I'm on the phone.'

Nothing new there. She was never off it.

'Can I come in a minute?'

141

He heard her talking into her mobile.

'Hold on, Becky, can you? It's my nuisance brother.'

The door to her room was jerked abruptly open. Marie stood in the doorway, her hair pinned up, her phone in her hand.

'Well?'

'Marie – can I talk to you a minute? It's about Dad . . .'

She looked at him with irritation, then put her phone back to her ear.

'Becky, I'll ring you back in five minutes. That okay? Okay. Speak to you then.' She ended the call. 'Well?'

'Can I come in?'

'All right. But don't touch anything. And make it quick. I'm going out.'

Marie's room was a mess, with clothes and books all over. Tom didn't understand why people thought girls were tidy. His sister certainly wasn't.

'Not there! Don't sit on my books!'

She moved them.

'All right. What is it?'

Tom unfolded the canvas and he held it out for her to take.

'Read that.'

She made no effort to take it.

'What is it? It stinks. It stinks of fish.'

'It's a message,' Tom said. 'About Dad.'

She stared at him, perhaps with a trace of anger in her eyes – annoyance, at least.

'What do you mean – a message? Who from?'

'I found it,' Tom said.

'Where?'

He was reluctant to say, but there wasn't a choice.

'In a bottle that I found. In the sea.'

Marie laughed – not as though anything was funny, but in a dismissive, derisory, slightly outraged way.

'What!'

'It was an experiment,' he explained. 'Something I just wanted to do. I put a message in a bottle. Ages ago. And then, a long time after, an answer came. So I wrote another message. And then this came today. You have to read it to understand. Here's the first message as well.'

He proffered both of the precious letters. The first message that he had hidden in his room had partially dried out. The ink on it, Tom noticed, was already fading, even though the canvas had been kept out of the light.

'Read that one first,' he said.

Marie looked at him with a superior, elder-sister sort of look. But as she read the messages, her face grew serious, troubled, then her expression turned to anger.

'Is this some sort of joke?'

Tom shook his head.

'I don't think this is funny, Tom,' Marie said. 'It's sick.'

'I found them,' Tom insisted. 'I'm not making it up. Dad's not dead, Marie. He's not dead!'

She stood up, very angry now, and she threw the pieces of canvas down upon the bed.

'Marie!' he cried, distraught. 'Don't do that!' He carefully retrieved them.

'For God's sake, Tom – is it you doing this? Is this some sort of . . . ? Is this some fantasy? Wishful thinking? I know you miss him – I do, Mum does, we all do. But stuff like this . . . this won't bring him back, Tom! What good is this?' Her anger turned to sympathy then; a more tender note came into her voice. 'Look, Tom, I do understand,' she said. 'I do . . .'

'No!' he yelled at her. 'That's just it, you don't! Don't get all big sister on me! Don't start all that! It isn't me, Marie. It isn't. It's not me at all. I didn't write them. They came from the sea. They did!'

She looked at him, expressionless, wondering . . .

'It's not me, Marie,' Tom said, his voice insistent, pleading, dying to be believed. 'It's not me.'

She went on staring at him, silent, unconvinced. He held both of the messages from the bottles in his hands. She felt a wave of compassion then, of sadness; he was her brother, after all. She even made a movement as if to put her arm around him, but as she did . . .

144

'Do you think . . . do you think I should tell Mum?' Tom said.

That did it. Marie erupted and lost control. There were feelings inside her she didn't even have names for. For a moment Tom thought she was going to strike him. Her face was right next to his and he could smell her breath. Flecks of spit came from her mouth. Her finger was held up in warning.

'Don't you *dare!*' she said. 'After everything she's been through. Don't you *dare* say that to her. How could you ever . . . ever . . . even think of being that cruel . . .'

'But, Marie, it says . . . it says he's not there . . . he's still here . . . still . . .'

'Tom, how can you be so stupid, so naive? It's a joke, can't you see? Someone's found the bottles you threw in and they're writing back this garbage for you to find. It's a joke. A sick, awful, terrible joke.'

Tom stared at her. This was a possibility he had not taken into account. Not that Ted Bones's second letter could be a pretence, a falsehood. He considered the possibility for half a second and then rejected it outright. No. No one would do that.

'But, Marie, what if there is an explanation? Only we don't understand how people . . .'

'No, Tom. There is no "what if". Dead people don't write letters from the bottom of the sea. It's

145

a sick, sick joke that someone's playing on you. That's all it is. A sick joke. And you must never show that to Mum. Ever. It would destroy her. You see? You promise?'

Tom felt tears coming to his eyes, but he fought them back. He nodded his head.

'You promise?'

'I promise,' he said. 'I promise.'

And then, to his astonishment, Marie did put her arms around him, and she held him so tight he felt that she would crush the air out of him and he would never be able to breathe again.

'Oh, Tom,' she said. 'Oh, Tom . . .'

And that was all she said, or needed to say, and he put his arms around her too, and they stood there for a few moments, then released each other, and they wiped their tears away.

He rolled up the pieces of canvas and tried to hide them in his hands. 'I'm sorry,' he said.

'It's not your fault,' she said. 'I just don't understand how anyone could do that . . . write that . . . be so . . . so cruel.'

'I'll . . . I'll . . .' He didn't really know what to say or do now. 'I'll . . . just leave it,' he said.

'Okay. I'd better ring Becky.'

'Okay. Sorry,' he said again, as he left her room.

'It's not your fault, Tom. Not your fault.'

146

He went back to his room and closed the door behind him.

It was his fault though, wasn't it? he thought. At least in some ways. He'd started it all, with that first letter in the bottle, that he had thrown into the sea. Quite innocently. Just for a bit of fun. And now it had turned into this.

He sat at his desk and re-read both of the messages. As he did, he felt a sense of anger and bitter injustice rise in him. Marie was right. Of course the letters couldn't be real. Someone was playing an unforgivable joke on him, pretending to be Ted Bones. And it was a terrible, awful thing to have done. To have written these things, to have made all this up, to tell him that his father was still alive when a whole year had gone by since his ship had sunk to the bottom of the sea.

He was going to find out who had done it. He wasn't going to let them get away with it. He'd find out who dared to mock their loss, and he'd shame them to the whole wide world.

147

16

BAIT

The thing was, Tom realised, whoever was finding these bottles, hadn't found them all. Because R.D. at school had found one, hadn't he? The one with the message from the aliens. While nobody seemed to have rescued the bottle with the *Dear Stupid* message inside it, or the *You Have Won the Lottery* one. What had happened to them? And to the bottle vase? The reject from his mother's studio. Were they still drifting round the oceans, or lying at the bottom of the sea? So how come so-called 'Ted Bones' had found some messages but not others? Was it simply down to luck? The flow of the tide? Or had some mysterious person been secretly watching Tom from the shelter of the cliffs, and plucking those bottles from the outgoing waves the moment Tom's back was turned? But who would do a thing like that?

That coming weekend, he went back to the estuary crossing to help Gareth out on the *King Billy* ferry. There was something restful about the back and forth over the river, something calming and reassuring in its dull monotony and repetition. Tom began to see what Gareth liked about it. It was all very well longing for change, but sometimes, when it came along, you just wanted things to go back to how they had been before. The same old same old had something comforting about it.

They got the fishing rods out when things were quiet, and draped a couple of lines over the side of the ferry, so as to fish as they went along. But they caught nothing, so after a while Gareth wound one of the lines in and replaced the bright silver spinner on the end of it with a baited hook. This time they caught a fish almost immediately. The spinners weren't attracting them, but fresh bait did.

'That's what they want today, eh, Tom? If you want to catch something, you just need the right bait.'

Yes. No doubt you did. *The right bait.* That *was* what you needed, Tom thought.

As the ferry zigzagged across the river from landing to landing, Tom looked up at each crossing to stare upstream towards the big ships at anchor in Rose Haven, still waiting for cargoes to carry and for orders to sail.

'They're still painting then, Uncle Gareth.'

'Be painting it the rest of their lives, if you ask me,' Gareth sneered. 'Suck the life out of you, a job like that.'

149

Sure enough the two distant men, one little, one large, were there at work, toiling away with sandpaper, rollers, brushes and pots, repainting the hull a newer, smarter grey. The cradle they worked from had moved along and they were slowly approaching the bows. In another week or so they would be around on the other side of the ship and working their way back towards the stern.

The ferry came in to Brent's Landing, and the big ships were lost from sight, back around the curve of the river.

The two men on the cradle worked on in silence. They didn't talk much. Their means of communication was limited to a few words in common. There were other problems too, as Keo well knew. His companion had difficulties. That fall of his, from a high deck to water, had left him injured and with his memory impaired. He'd struck his head on something in the sea – a floating oil drum, a piece of wood perhaps. He'd stare at you sometimes, with a blank, empty look on his face, as if he didn't know you or recognise you, or understand where you both were or what you were doing there.

'You okay, Charlie?' Keo would ask.

Charlie would look at him, as if trying to place him, to recall how the two of them came to be on that huge ship in that quiet haven, dangling in a cradle from the deck high above them, painting the world grey.

'You okay, Charlie? You all right?'

The perplexity would lift then, and a faint smile would cross the big man's face.

'I'm okay. You okay, Keo?'

'Okay, Charlie. We both okay.'

And so, this having been established, the two of them would work on, sanding, cleaning, rubbing down, applying paint, until finally it was break time.

Then, 'We go up now, Charlie – okay? Brew some tea?'

The big man would nod, and between them they would carefully manoeuvre the cradle upwards by means of the pulleys, and have twenty minutes to themselves.

Bait. That was what Tom needed. Just as Uncle Gareth had said – the way to lure things out into the open was by tempting them with something irresistible. Only Tom had bigger fish to catch than mackerel – he was after fish that weren't fish at all.

So yes, cast your bread upon the waters, thought Tom that evening, but this time stay and watch and wait. Stay and hide and keep looking, and see what happens. See who comes for the bottle, who rises to take the bait.

Who was it who pretended to be old Ted Bones? Who gave themselves the authority to say that Tom's dad, Samuel Pellow, was not with his shipmates at the bottom of the sea? When it had been over a year now since his ship had been lost; since a letter had come from the shipping company; since the compensation had been paid; since those useless, meaningless apologies had been made – none of which would ever bring him back.

The right bait would help to answer that question. The right lure on the right barbed hook. That was the way to catch the fish you were after; that was how to reel it in – with a little cunning and temptation.

Dear Mr Bones,

I found your message and read what it said, but I find it hard to believe it is true and feel there must be a mistake. You say that nobody called Samuel Pellow is with you, but that really can't be so, as his boat was lost and went down with all hands, and no one was saved at all. It was in all the papers and there was a big enquiry, and that was over a year ago.

Maybe, Mr Bones, you could tell me a little more about yourself – like how you find my messages and how you reply? Are you really at the bottom of the sea? Or are you somewhere else? I don't want to be rude or to sound suspicious, but I do wonder, Mr Bones, if maybe you are not just pretending. I wonder if you are Mr Ted Bones at all, but someone else – someone still here and on dry land.

So how do you find my messages, Mr Bones? Luck might find one of them – but to find two sounds like more than luck. How do you do it, Mr Bones? For the ocean is a great big place, and a bottle is a tiny thing.

Please write back, if you would, and tell me how you can be so sure about Samuel Pellow, for, to be honest, Mr Bones, it would be a very cruel thing to tell someone that a person is still here in the world when he is not, and when they have already gone through so much.

I do try to think that you are a good, kind soul, Mr Bones, and wouldn't deliberately hurt anyone's feelings. But some things are very hard to believe, especially when you know otherwise.

Maybe, if you know of some explanation, you might write back to let me know what it is.

Sincerely, your message-in-a-bottle penfriend,
Tom Pellow

Tom read the message through. As soon as he did, he saw ways to improve it. Yet he didn't change a word.

It would do. It would have to do. Imperfect as it was, it was adequate. There was no sense in elaborating or trying to put things differently or to phrase them better. The message got the message across. That was what mattered. And it wasn't too strong. It wasn't angry. It even had a forgiving tone to it – allowing room for an apology, for Ted Bones to admit that a mistake had been made, and no hard feelings.

What Ted Bones – or so-called Ted Bones – wouldn't know was that Tom would be watching this time. He'd be up there on Needle Rock with the binoculars, hiding behind the Smokestack, watching the bottle as the waves carried it out to sea.

Tom would be watching this time, to see who came for it; to see the hand rise from the water, grasp the bottle, and take it down perhaps.

Or, more likely, Tom would see something else. Like the real, the mundane, the plausible, logical explanation. He might see an all too solid someone in an all too solid boat, plucking the bottle from the water, with a furtive look on their face and a sly smile. Yes, he had his suspicions as to what he might witness – and soon now he would take the opportunity to confirm them.

On Sunday Marie was at her friend's house and Tom's mother was making pots and keeping an ear out for

154

the bell ringing in the shop, in case customers appeared.

'Just going for a walk, Mum, down to the harbour and around.'

'All right,' she said. 'But be . . .'

He knew. Careful. Be careful. No need to say.

'See you later.'

'Bye, Tom.'

He left – the binoculars in his backpack, along with the glass bottle, sealed tight, the message inside.

He circled the harbour, took the coastal path, and climbed to Needle Rock. The gulls were there, as ever, perching, swooping, floating on the wind, wings wide as they sailed like kites out over the sea.

Tom sat and waited, perched on the rock, looking down at the black depths of the sea and the white caps of the breakers, foaming as water swirled around stone.

He waited for an hour, maybe more. The tide slackened, turned. Tom had brought a sandwich with him and some squash. He sat, ate, drank, went on waiting. He raised the binoculars to his eyes and looked out to sea. He saw trawlers coming in; small pleasure craft turning for the harbour; an oil tanker far out on the horizon.

The afternoon became evening and the tide started to ebb. A mist formed, carried in by a light breeze. The marker buoy tolled its bell, as if in endless mourning for the lost and the dead.

Finally, feeling the moment was right and the tide favourable, Tom reached and took the bottle from his backpack. He checked that the stopper was properly secured. He placed the bottle down, picked up some stones, and had a practice throw with them. Then he took the bottle again, held it by the neck, drew back his arm and hurled it into the sea, as far away as he could.

He saw the splash. Keeping his gaze fixed on that patch of water he raised the binoculars to his eyes and focused them in. There it was. There was his bottle, bobbing in the water, drifting out with the current.

Tom stepped behind the Smokestack to conceal himself. He rested the binoculars upon a ledge of rock. He was hidden now. No one would see him, not if someone was indeed out there, watching. His hands were steady, but his pulse was racing.

He held the binoculars to his eyes and did his best to keep the bottle in sight, though it wasn't easy, for sometimes it disappeared under a wave, or into a swirl of dark water, and would reappear somewhere else, and he had to search for it.

Out it drifted. The minutes passed. The quarter-hour. The half. But still he held it in view. It was getting smaller though and harder to see. Soon it would be gone from sight. His neck was aching; his arms too; his hands were growing cold.

The mist was still moving in across the water and

thickening as it came. Daylight was fast ebbing with the tide and the sunset was on its way. There it was now, dusk, just beginning, huge and red and breathtaking.

Tom kept the lenses of the binoculars trained on the bottle all the while. He could still see it, but only just. No hand had appeared to seize it; no ghost had come to spirit it away to the deep. No sign of anyone or anything.

But then . . .

Then . . .

From the mist and darkness, suddenly, silently appearing, as if coming from nowhere, or from some other dimension.

A boat. A small boat, a row boat. And a figure upon it, swathed in heavy clothes against the cold, with a hat pulled down tight over their brow.

On the row boat came, out of the mist. Its occupant rowed steadily, swiftly and strongly. The man at the oars seemed to know where he was going.

Tom watched. Trying to recognise the figure, trying to make out the name on the prow of the boat. What did it say? And that shape, that man alone in the boat, and the boat itself, they both seemed eerily familiar, as if Tom knew them already, and had done, all his life. They were like dredged-up memories, clouded visions of the past.

157

Where was it headed? Where was this boat going, alone in the water, in the descending mist and darkness? No one would go out in that sea, not in a flimsy rowing boat, on the outgoing tide, in these conditions. It would be asking for trouble.

But the man rowed determinedly on, as if he knew just where he was heading, and just what he had to do.

The boat was heading for the bottle.

Tom forgot the cold of his hands and the discomfort of his hiding place. His elbows dug into the rocks as he craned nearer, but he didn't feel their sharpness.

Who was in the boat? Who?

It looked a bit like Stovey from a distance. The figure was all wrapped up, yes, but it looked like him – his shape and build. It looked like his boat too. Yet it couldn't be. Not Stovey. Stovey would never have written a message like that one, making out Tom's dad was still alive when he was dead. They had known each other, gone out on the trawlers together. Stovey would never do that.

But who then?

What did that name on the prow of the boat say? Why was the lettering so faded and spidery, so eroded by wind and weather and time and the sea?

Look, look.

The man had ceased rowing. He was pulling one of the oars in and using the other to turn the boat around.

158

He was level with the bottle now. *See – see.* He was stopped right by it. There. Now look – he had it in his hand, scooped out of the water, and then it was in the boat, and both oars were back in the sea, and he was rowing away, like a man pursued, like a man on the run, with sharks after him – man-eaters, their mouths open, their teeth like knives.

But the sheer speed at which he rowed was impossible, and against the tide too. No man could row like that. Yet on he went, unstoppable, implacable, it seemed. He went back the way he had come, into the thickening mist and the descending darkness. The sun was low on the horizon now, but its light suddenly flared up and shone straight into the binocular lenses. Tom blinked and momentarily looked away. Then he put the glasses back to his eyes. But the boat and the man had gone. And the bottle had gone with them. All three had vanished into mist and sea and darkness.

Tom emerged from behind the Smokestack. No need to hide now. He scanned the sea from left to right and back. But there was nothing. No one.

He looked at the time on his watch and realised that he should be turning for home. But all the same, just a few more minutes . . .

He stared and stared, but could see nothing. Only mist, spray, grey and ochre sky, dark running sea.

Who had been in the boat? Had it been Stovey?

But it couldn't have been. And the name on the prow. That wasn't the name of Stovey's boat. It wasn't the name of anyone's boat. There was no boat of that name anywhere in Delwick harbour, not that Tom knew of, and he knew them all.

He stood and watched and watched and watched. He thought of a dozen explanations but could believe in none of them. Some explanations he yearned to believe, and others he feared to. Some had reason to them, and others only faith and hope, and no other foundation.

At length, he heard his phone ringing, and he quickly answered it.

'Sorry, Mum, I lost track of the time. I'm all right though. I'm on my way back. I'm coming home right now.'

He walked down the path, sure-footed, even in darkness, he knew it so well. He'd walked it many times. Down the path to the harbour. Stovey's rowing boat, Tom saw, was on the harbour wall, up on blocks, still undergoing maintenance and small repairs. His inflatable dinghy was tied to a metal ring by the steps, and his cabin cruiser was languishing on the mud.

Tom turned up the hill to home. The lights were on in the Anchor Inn. Some trawlermen were in there, also at anchor for a while. Tom saw Stovey inside, with a glass in his hand, deep in conversation.

Not Stovey then. Someone else. Some unknown stranger who had appeared from the mist and vanished back into it as rapidly and silently as he had come.

And he had taken the bottle. That had been his purpose and his sole intention. He had rowed out of the darkness, just to pick the bottle out of the water and to take the message away.

Ted Bones, Tom thought. Was it old Ted Bones?

He shuddered. But then he told himself not to be so ridiculous. How could dead men come to you from the bottom of the sea?

17

SWAN OF EVE

The *Swan of Eve* . . .

That had been the name on the prow of the boat that the phantom figure had rowed across the turbulent sea.

The *Swan of Eve*.

Tom knew the name from somewhere yet he could not quite place it. It was annoying to have the name there, like a word on the tip of your tongue, that you could so nearly, but not quite, pronounce. He brooded over the name all through Monday's lessons, his mind unable to concentrate on anything else. But the answer wouldn't come. He needed someone or something to jog his memory. That evening, after school, he walked down to the harbour.

'Stovey . . .'

Stovey looked up from his carpentry to see Tom Pellow standing by him. Stovey's row boat was much improved. There was new wood skilfully cut into it, replacing sections of rotten planking.

'All right, Tom? Another day of school done with then? One more step closer to freedom?'

162

Stovey had left school at fourteen and had gone straight to work at the fish market. After two years of that, he was out on the trawlers, and had spent the next fifty years pulling fish out of the water and managing to stay alive while keeping most of his limbs intact. Stovey had never been much of a one for studying.

'I guess so,' Tom said. He didn't mind school. At least he wasn't in a hurry to leave. He hesitated, reluctant to get to the point. 'What are you doing?' he asked, by way of conversation.

'What's it look like?' Stovey asked back, by way of mild sarcasm.

'Fixing your boat.'

'That'd be right then,' Stovey said, and he took up the wood plane he had been using and smoothed away some splinters.

'Stovey . . .'

'What's up, boy?' he said. Not like Tom here not to get to the point.

'You know all the boats round here, don't you, Stovey?'

'I should do by this time. You must know most of them yourself, don't you?'

'I thought so.' Tom tried to seem relaxed, as if he were just idling away the time. 'But I saw one last night I didn't recognise.'

'Probably just passing by,' Stovey grunted, with a

163

blatant lack of interest. 'Can't know all the boats in the world, can you?'

'No, it had to be moored up nearby. Someone was rowing it. Last night, just around dusk.'

Stovey stopped working and stared at him.

'Out rowing? With it getting dark and the mist coming in? He must have had an outboard, surely?'

'No, it didn't. It was a row boat. Oars and no engine. I saw it from the rock.'

'What were you doing up there with it getting dark then?'

'Oh, nothing.'

'Nothing? Right. I see. So tell me, Tom,' Stovey said with an affected air of curiosity. 'What sort of "nothing" was it that you were getting up to? Or would you rather not say?'

'Oh, you know,' Tom said vaguely, '. . . just . . . nothing in particular. I had the binoculars with me. Sort of bird spotting, really.'

'Oh yeah?' Stovey put the plane down and took up a sanding block. Tom hated the noise it made. It set him on edge.

'And that was when I saw the boat. It was a tender . . .'

Stovey looked up again.

'A tender?'

'You know, the small row boat that a big ship

would have for getting in to harbour when they're out at anchor.'

'I know what a tender is, boy. I ought to at my age.'

'No, I just meant . . . I mean, the thing is . . . they have the same name, don't they? The tender and the ship. A lot of the time. Like, if a ship's called the *Dolphin*, say, then the small boat would have *Tender to the Dolphin* on the prow, wouldn't it?'

'And so?' Stovey said, wondering where, if anywhere, all this was leading. 'It's a nautical education listening to you, Tom,' he added, with even more pointed sarcasm than before.

'Well, that was what I saw last night,' Tom said. 'I saw this row boat come out of the mist, and it was a tender, and it had the name of the mother ship painted on the side, and I wondered if you might know it, because I'm sure I've heard of it before, but I can't quite remember where.'

'And it was?' Stovey said, putting down the sanding block and wiping down his boat's hull with a cloth to get the wood dust off.

'Well, it was quite foggy and it was getting dark, and I might have been mistaken . . . as the lettering on the side was very faded . . .'

'Tom – if you have a point, will you get to it? If not, I'm off home for my tea.'

'No, it's just . . . well, as far as I could make out,

the name on the side was *Swan of Eve*. That was what it said. It said in small letters *Tender to*, then in bigger ones *Swan of Eve*.

Stovey stopped working. He straightened up. He moved as though his back were creaking, but it didn't make any noise that Tom could hear.

'*Swan of Eve?*'

'Yes.'

Stovey narrowed his eyes.

'Tom, boy,' he said. 'Are you taking the mickey?'

Tom coloured and felt hot.

'No. Why do you say that?'

'Tom, what do you know about the place here? Don't they teach you about your own home at school these days? Or do you just learn about abroad, like local means nothing?'

'A bit. We've done the fishing industry, mining, tin, coal . . .'

'No, no, I mean here, right *here*. Delwick. Where we're standing. Now, you see the warning light out there, past the sign? That one at the end of the harbour?'

'Yes.'

'Hasn't always been there, has it? Do you reckon?'

'I suppose not.'

'No. No one puts a light up till there's a reason for it. No one's going to warn you about dangerous rocks until a few ships start hitting them. And then, when

166

a few have gone down, someone thinks of putting a warning light up, and a couple of buoys with bells on them – so a skipper'll know there's trouble ahead, even if he can't see it yet, he'll hear it coming.'

'Yes? And so . . . ?'

'Have you ever read the information board, up by the end of the harbour, next to the memorial?' Stovey asked him.

'I think so,' replied Tom, feeling uncertain.

'Well you should go and have another look,' Stovey said. 'You might find the answer to your question.'

'Okay . . .' Tom looked hesitantly towards the end of the harbour wall. Large waves were smashing over it, and sea spray plumed into brief rainbows.

Stovey sighed. 'You go look at the history board, Tom.'

Tom tried to swallow. His mouth felt dry. He remembered now. He clearly recollected where he had seen the name before. He had seen it right there, in the list of shipwrecks – the oldest and the first recorded.

'Is the *Swan of Eve* on there? It is, isn't it?'

'She hit the rocks more than two hundred years ago, boy. It was one of the worst storms ever, according to parish records – though who knows how accurate they are. The local men went out to try and rescue who they could. They found just three survivors. The rest all perished. The ship broke up in the storm, and

167

what remains of it – if anything – is still lying out there somewhere, at the bottom of the sea.'

'But . . .'

'So if you think you saw a tender belonging to the *Swan of Eve* last night, Tom, then I think you might need a visit to the optician. And while you're there, ask if he's got my glasses. Because you're a little bit late to be seeing the *Swan of Eve*, mate. About two hundred years too late.'

Stovey looked at him, a faint smile on his face and a quizzical eyebrow raised.

'Yes, but, Stovey, I mean, isn't it possible . . . couldn't there be another boat, another ship, with the same name? That could happen, couldn't it?'

'It could. But if you saw it last night, then where is it? If you saw the tender, then the ship itself had to be at anchor nearby. And where was that, Tom? You see any ships at anchor last night?'

Tom slowly shook his head.

'I was out myself yesterday afternoon, on my crabber,' Stovey told him, 'bringing the pots in. There was nothing out there then, Tom. Coast was clear and the sea was too. So I don't know what you saw, mate, but it wasn't no *Swan of Eve*.'

Tom wanted to get away now. It didn't matter what Stovey said. He *had* seen the boat. Yes, the light had been failing, and yes, the writing on the prow of the boat had been faint and spidery and faded and hard to make out. But he had made it out, and he knew what he had seen.

Tender to the Swan of Eve – that *was* what it had said. And there had been no outboard motor on the boat. Not even the fittings and brackets for one.

'I must have been mistaken,' Tom said, just to smooth things over. 'I must have seen something else.'

Stovey wiped his hands with the rag he held and started putting his tools and brushes away.

'You must have been, Tom. But I can't think what you did see then. I can't think who'd be reckless enough to go out in a small row boat, in the fog and dark, for no good reason. I mean, what was he up to? Where was he heading?'

'I . . . I don't know,' Tom said. 'I guess . . . I don't know. Maybe . . . he was . . . looking for something.'

'You ever heard of such a thing, Tom, as an overactive imagination?'

Tom felt his face grow hot again. It wasn't embarrassment this time; it was annoyance.

'I did see it, Stovey! I saw a boat. I was standing right there, by the Smokestack. I saw it quite clearly.'

'Then you must be seeing ghosts, mate,' Stovey said with a chuckle. 'That's all I can think – that you must be seeing ghosts. And for someone who don't even believe in mermaids, that seems a bit strange to me.'

'It was real,' Tom said. 'There was a man on board, rowing for all he was worth. As real as you and me. And he stopped and reached out and he took . . .'

Tom stopped abruptly. He had said too much. In his anger he had said far more than he wanted to.

'He stopped and took what?' Stovey said – intrigued but doubtful, slightly mocking too, cynical.

'He took . . . I don't know . . . something out of the water.'

'Like what? I hope he wasn't pinching one of my crab pots. If so, I'll be looking for him myself.'

'I don't know. I just . . . saw him take something . . . that was all.'

Stovey sighed. His gear was packed up now; he was ready to go home.

'Tom,' he said, 'you go brooding too much, boy. The sea's like a crystal ball, see – you stare at it long enough, you see all sorts of things in it, that maybe aren't there, things that are just imaginings. I know you've all had bad times, you and your sister and your mum, but we've got to go on, Tom. The past isn't a thing to ever forget, but it's not something to dwell on too much neither. There's not a family in the village hasn't known the same. Every one of us, Tom, at some time or another. That's the penalty of living here. There's the good and there's the grim. That's the price of making a living from the sea. It's a high one, and let's hope it never has to be paid again. But we've got to carry on, Tom – there's no choice. The trawlers've still got to go out every morning. The fish won't catch themselves.'

Stovey looked at him for some kind of response.

'I know,' was all Tom could think to say. 'I know.' And he did. But so what if he did? He also knew what he had seen the night before; and he knew he had read those letters from old Ted Bones. He had held them in his hands.

'You go careful,' Stovey said. He took up his belongings and he left.

Tom remained where he was, at the harbour side. He sat on Stovey's upturned row boat, and looked out to sea, towards the light at the tip of the harbour wall and to the expanse of ocean beyond.

'I did,' he whispered to himself. 'The *Swan of Eve*. I did see it. I did.'

He sat for a few minutes, lost in thought, then rose and walked along the harbour wall to where the information board stood, with a brief history of the village on display, for the benefit of tourists. The wind had dropped now and the waves had calmed.

There was a drawing printed upon the board, behind laminated plastic, in pen and ink: an artist's impression of the *Swan of Eve*. It was many masted and under full sail, as if riding a storm. It dragged a small boat behind it, a small rowing boat, a tender, which danced on the waves as it went along. It looked like a child of some sort, following its mother – like a lamb behind a sheep.

I saw that boat come out of the mist, Tom thought. I did see it. I did.

He reached up to the drawing and traced the shape of the boat with his fingers, then he looked out to the rocks, upon which so many boats had floundered over the years.

Someone had taken the bottle from the sea. He had seen them do so with his own eyes. Only who? And when would he get an answer?

Yes, Tom thought, anyone could put a message in a bottle and throw it into the sea. There was nothing so unusual about that. But when the sea started writing back to you – that was different, that was special, that was weird and strange and wonderful. And even a little terrifying.

A wave crashed against the harbour wall, and spray fell upon him like a shower of rain. He could taste the salt on his lips and feel the dampness in his hair. But he made no effort to walk away. The sea, for all its roughness, felt like a friend to him now. If you lingered, and if you didn't mind its swells and sulks and temper, it might reveal itself, and confide in you – tell you all its secrets.

A second, larger wave broke, and this time it soaked him through. But Tom didn't mind; he really didn't mind. The sea is in us all. It is where we come from.

172

18

YOURS, AS ALWAYS . . .

The days went by and Tom wished there were someone he could confide in, but he felt that there was no one.

Whom could he tell? Not his mother, nor his sister either. Not now, not after the last time. Marie would get annoyed with him again, and tell him not to be so naive and stupid. When there was something that couldn't be explained or easily understood, people always told you not to be so stupid – as if that answered the question.

But who would believe him? Who would ever accept that a small boat, which had gone down to the bottom of the sea two centuries ago, had appeared from the mist, with a long-dead crew man at the oars, rowing for all he was worth, to snatch a bottle from the water and to disappear as swiftly as he had come, back into the swirling mist?

How to explain the inexplicable? Where was the sense, the logic, the rational explanation? Yet there had to be one, surely.

What about Uncle Gareth? Tom thought. Perhaps

he could tell him. But, on reflection, he soon decided against it. Gareth wouldn't believe a word.

'You been doing a bit too much homework there, have you, Tom, boy? Bit too much of that studying?' he'd probably say. 'You'll do your brains in, mate, doing too much of that. You'll start seeing things – well, to be honest, mate, it sounds like you already have.'

There was nobody, Tom realised, that he could turn to – or, at least, no one who would believe him if he did. Maybe he could go to church, kneel down on one of the worn and fraying hassocks and confide in you-know-who. But Tom wasn't sure about you-know-who. For wasn't you-know-who supposed to be infinitely good and powerful? And yet he let people drown in the sea. Tom didn't know that he altogether trusted the idea of you-know-who.

Or perhaps he could tell someone at school. R.D., maybe, who believed in aliens and monsters from outer space and bottles that couldn't break. But R.D. was gullible enough to believe anything. He'd be no help at all.

There was just him. It had only been him from the start. He had thrown a bottle into the sea and this was the outcome of that simple act. What goes around comes around. Wasn't that what people said? Things can come back to bite you too. Every deed, every thought even, has consequences, some people said. And what if they were right?

There was just waiting now, that was all. So Tom waited, and he watched, hoping for a reply to the last letter he had committed to the sea. He went down to the harbour every morning, and he walked up to Needle Rock every afternoon, and each weekend he went to help out at the estuary crossing by Rose Haven – for the answer might drift in there.

He usually carried the binoculars with him, just in case. And he was always looking, perpetually looking, for a shiny glimpse of a sun-struck gleam of glass, reflecting from the water. He was a prospector, a miner – a miner of the sea. One day he'd strike gold again; he'd find the diamond, the gem, the glittering prize of green glass. And inside would be the words to explain everything.

It was bobbing on the water out there, even now, waiting for a favourable current. It would be drawn to him, as if by magnetism, by some instinct – the way a migrating bird could fly five thousand miles, yet still, with no map or compass, always find its way home.

It'll come, Tom thought. It'll come. He willed it to. He believed it to. His belief alone would surely make it come. Where logic failed, faith might yet triumph. He would make the message come to him, he would. He would.

But still it didn't.

One week. Two more. Three.

The half-term break, and then it was gone. Tests, exams, days out, museum visits, trips, excursions. The clocks changing; the lengthening days. The Patchwork Tea Shoppe in Delwick Cove, which stayed closed in the off season, reopened. The shutters came down from its windows; the cakes appeared on stands; the first of the tourists arrived to eat them.

What a picturesque place. What a charming village. Wouldn't it be lovely to live here? Have a summer hideaway, maybe? A little cottage.

And the trawlermen on the harbour, sitting mending their nets, would look at the tourists – not unkindly, but with a grim amusement, thinking to themselves of the winter bitterness and the December storms and the January chill – of ice on the harbour wall and of their frozen hands at a dark four a.m. of the morning, as they set out into the teeth of a howling wind to fish for cod, and to eke out from the sea no more than a basic living for all their efforts.

Nice little place, eh? Be nice to have a summer cottage? Maybe, if you had the money, and could afford to winter in the Bahamas.

The evenings lightened. Tom more frequently took his board down to the beach after school and joined the surfers there. He wasn't a great surfer, but he could balance and stand up on the board all right and ride the breakers a decent distance before tumbling into the sea. R.D. floundered clumsily among them all, half boy, half ungainly walrus.

Latterly Tom liked to paddle out on his board, just beyond the surf break, to a point where the incoming waves were still smooth and glassy and hadn't yet burst into white-capped surf.

He'd drift and bob and watch and look. The water got into his eyes sometimes and the salt stung, and you couldn't rub them then, for that just made things worse. You had to let them water, and allow the tears to wash the salt away. Sometimes there were jellyfish, which gave him the creeps. He always steered the board to avoid them if he could. Not that he'd ever been stung – not yet.

Then one day he finally saw it. Through a blur of tears. He blinked and blinked again. Then he kicked his feet as he lay on the board, and propelled it over to where he had glimpsed the flash of light.

It had gone. He must have been wrong.

But no. The waves surged and carried it up, and there it was again. Emerald green, shiny and bright. Tom splashed towards it and reached out with his hand. He had it. *The* bottle. The bottle that he had waited for, for so long now.

177

He held it tight. His feet splashed in the water as he turned the board around. He crossed the break line, where the waves turned to surf. He grabbed a wave and stood up on the board, arms out, the bottle held tightly in his right hand, and he rode the wave in to the beach.

'Hey, Tom! You going already?' called Ryan. 'Won't be dark for another hour.'

Tom waved at his friend and shouted back.

'Got stuff to do!' he called, doing his best to keep the bottle concealed behind his board. He didn't want anyone else becoming curious.

'Later then!'

'Yeah. Maybe tomorrow.'

'See you!'

'See you!'

Tom headed for home. It wasn't far. People strolling through the streets in wetsuits with surfboards under their arms were a common enough sight.

He got in and left the board in the shed, then changed and hosed the wetsuit down with fresh water and hung it on the line to dry. He could hear the sound of the pottery wheel spinning. His mother was still at work.

'Back, Mum!' he called.

'How was it?'

'Great,' he said. 'Cold, but great.'

'Just be half an hour or so.'

178

'Okay.'

He went to his room and held the bottle to the light. There it was. He could see it. A rolled, ragged piece of canvas, just as before.

Round and round the ragged rocks the ragged rascal ran.

Stupid really, the things you thought of sometimes.

She sells sea shells on the sea . . .

He unscrewed the cap. He inserted his little finger, got a grip upon the piece of tightly rolled canvas, and gradually pulled it out through the neck of the bottle.

Damp and fishy smelling. Just as before. Tom flattened it upon the surface of the desk. He saw those same thin, spidery letters, half written upon, half scratched into, the sallow strip of canvas.

Tom found himself not wanting to read what it said. A feeling of dread eclipsed his curiosity. What if it contained fresh news and revelations that he didn't want to hear? He suddenly wished he hadn't found it. He wished he'd never started this whole thing. Why had he ever thought it would be a good idea, to cast a message into the sea?

But there was no going back.

He looked down at the canvas and at the first words written upon it, in that old-fashioned, quaint, italic script.

Dear Shipmate . . .

Tom shuddered. As if someone had walked over his grave. But the feeling passed. And he read on.

I be in receipt of your most recent correspondence. Which I have to say perturbed
me greatly. For, rest assured, my dear shipmate, that Ted Bones would never play a man
false, nor give him information that he knew
not to be so. A sailor is a sailor and he
would never do down a shipmate. For don't
us sea-going men all face the same hardships
and misfortunes and difficult ways?

All I can say is that I have made enquiries
both long and deep, throughout the length
and breadth of this place us lost souls call
home. I mean down here in what we call Davy
Jones's Locker – though you may call it what
you will and no difference.

There ain't no Samuel Pellow here, shipmate,
and that's the truth. What I'm thinking is
that maybe he travelled under a different
name – which ain't so unusual. There's many a
seafaring man has had reason to change his
name. My own name now, wasn't always Ted
Bones. Ted Bones ain't a name you've born

with see; it's just who you end up being due to circumstances.

So what I'm meaning, see, is that if anyone went enquiring for me under that old marker of mine, back before I changed it, they might not find no news, as that old self of mine has gone.

Maybe this Sam Pellow, he sailed under another name too. Maybe that explains why I can't give you no news. Maybe when he sailed, he went under the title of Sam the Rover, or Sam Salt, or anything akin to that. I'm not saying it's so, just supposing.

But if that ain't the case, then he ain't here, shipmate. And if you're sure he's gone, then it's dry land you want to be looking at, not in watery depths. It's not a sailor's end he's had, see, shipmate. It would be a land-lubbing one.

It's sorry I am that I can't bring ye no better news, but that's the way of it, I'm afeared, for us all.

You take care now, shipmate, and don't ye get too taken over about things and go growing melancholy in your spirits. You're with the quick and living, matey, and that's what you need to be thinking on, and living it best you can.

181

So I'll bid ye farewell. I don't think I can help ye no more with news, shipmate, much as I'd like. You write back to old Ted Bones if things is still heavy on your mind. But I don't think I'll be able to give ye any different tidings – though I wishes as I could.

Go steady, shipmate. You just batten down the hatches tight, and ride out the storms which are bound to come, and then you'll see 'em through and come out all right at the other side. If the sun can shine one time, then the sun can shine again.

Safe sailing and fine weather.

Yours as always,

Ted Bones

Tom put down the letter. His eyes were full of tears again. But this time it was not the salt.

19
LAST ONE

The fact was that Tom's dad had only ever had one name: the name of Samuel Pellow. There was no mistaking him for anyone else and it didn't matter what Ted Bones said. Maybe it was to his lost and so deeply missed father that Tom should have written all along, and maybe, in truth, it was always really him to whom all those bottles had been addressed.

So one more then. Just one more. One more letter and then an end. Maybe it was the letter he should have written first – the reason he had written any of them. Maybe this was the letter that he had wanted to send to the sea all along.

Why had he not said what he had ached to, right from the beginning? Why not write the truth, even if it hurt, even if it seemed to wreck you from inside?

Tom took a pen and the notepad and he began to write.

Dear Dad,
  Ted Bones says you aren't out there in the sea,

but I know you are, despite all he says, so I'm writing to you, though I know it's a letter you will never read and never find.

I just want you to know that we're all okay and that we are managing. Mum is still making her pots and selling most of them too, and Marie will be going to university later in the year, like you wanted her to.

We all miss you and always will. I wish we had a place to visit, but we don't. Only the sea. So the sea is the place I always go to, and I write letters to it, and somehow it writes back, even though it says things that I can't believe.

Anyway, this is just to let you know that we think of you always and you will never be forgotten.

I help Uncle Gareth out on the ferry sometimes, and he always talks about you, every time. I don't think he can help it. Everyone remembers you.

So that's all.

This bottle might sail around the world for ever, I guess. But that won't matter, as it will always be there to remind me of you. It will be like a memorial – at least that's how I see it. My memorial in the sea.

I think of you often and I always will. I'll never forget you as long as I live. If I wrote

everything I feel, Dad, I would fill a thousand
bottles. I don't think there's room for all I feel
and all I have to say. There aren't enough bottles
in the world, Dad, or enough bits of paper.

Bye, Dad.
Love for ever,
Tom

There. It was done now. Said and done. Nobody else
would ever know – or ever need to. Let the sea take
your secrets and carry them away. Let them float around
the world for ever, found or unfound. But let them be
there, in perpetuity; in honour, in memory, in love.

What had Ted Bones said? Tom tried to recall. Oh
yes: *You're with the quick and living, matey, and that's*
what you need to be thinking on, and living it best
you can . . . If the sun can shine one time, then the
sun can shine again.

Tom sealed the cap tightly and hid the bottle in his
drawer. Tomorrow he would take it up to Needle Rock
and commit his last and final message to the sea. No
more after that. He'd be done. He'd said what he
wanted to. What answer could the sea give now? There
was none to give, no more to be said.

Maybe, until now, Tom had gone on hoping, but
finally, he had let those hopes go and had accepted
what he had so long denied.

Samuel Pellow was never coming back. That was it. The brutal truth.

'Out? Now? What for? It'll be dark in half an hour,' his mother said.

'I think I left one of my gloves down on the beach yesterday,' Tom explained. 'Just want to go and look for it. Probably dropped it by the rocks when I came out from surfing.'

The neoprene gloves kept his hands warm. After ten minutes in the winter sea, he could sometimes barely feel them. Even the summer waters came with a chill.

He didn't go to the beach though. He hid the bottle under his coat, left the house and headed up to Needle Rock.

He felt that there should have been some kind of ceremony, some means of lending solemnity and adding dignity to the proceedings – a few words, a prayer, a gesture, a brief silence. Or maybe just a sense that the moment was right.

He stood a while, looking out to sea, watching the tide go out and the night come in. Then, finally, he raised the bottle with the last and final message inside, and he threw it far into the ocean.

Then he stood, and waited, and watched.

Nothing. Only the sound of the sea; the darkness descending.

He turned to go, but then, as he did he heard something – the splash of wooden blades upon the lapping sea, the faint creak of ancient timber.

Looking out and towards the headland, Tom saw the boat again, the small row boat, its oars beating the water as it headed for the bottle that bobbed in the waves.

He watched, transfixed, without fear, simply engrossed, compelled, as if all this were happening to somebody else, and he was merely a spectator at someone else's drama.

He realised that he had forgotten the binoculars. The boat was hard to make out in the twilight, but it appeared to be the same figure as before at the oars, rowing with the same steady, almost inhuman, untiring determination.

The boat progressed through the water. Tom shouted out at it, angry and loud, no longer detached but involved now, every part and fibre of him absorbed in the moment.

'No!' he said. 'It isn't for you. The message isn't meant for you, it's for him!'

But the wind carried his words away and the noise of the sea drowned them. The man at the oars did not look up, but continued rowing. He was closing in upon the bottle, where it floated on the tide. Just as before, the boat slowed as it drew level. Tom watched, transfixed, half angry, half afraid. The man in the boat rested one of the oars along the planks, and he reached out to take the bottle from the water. His hand appeared to have no flesh upon it; it was just bones.

Tom wished he had the binoculars. He wished he could see the man's face. But maybe it was best that he couldn't. Maybe the face was as skeletal as the man's hands, and not a face at all, just a shrunken, eyeless, fleshless skull, hidden under the hat.

The claw that was the man's hand reached out to pluck the bottle from the water, but then it hesitated, and slowly withdrew. It was as if the man knew that the message was for someone else; that it was not for the eyes of strangers.

Tom stood by the Smokestack. But he wasn't hidden like before, he was visible and exposed. The boat was – what? – a few hundred yards from him, that was all. There it floated, the darkness thickening around it. The figure at the oars turned its head and looked towards the land. His eyes – if they were eyes, for Tom could not be sure if they were eyes or empty sockets – looked in his direction. They looked straight at him. More than that. Into him. It felt as though they could see inside him, into his very depths.

Tom's heart raced. His stomach twisted. It was as if he were looking into the face of death itself.

They watched each other, the boy on the land, and

the man – if it was a man – in the boat. Tom's fear abated. He watched as the figure in the boat raised its skeletal, sepulchral hand in greeting. The gesture, far from threatening, was kindly, sympathetic.

Tom felt his own arm rise into the air, as if by its own volition.

Was that a smile? A faint, pale, ghostly glimmer of a skeletal smile from under the brim of the dark, black hat?

Tom heard his own voice ring through the air, through the darkness and the spray of the water and over the salt of the sea.

'Is it you, Mr Bones? Is it you? It's me, Tom. Who writes the letters. Is it you, Mr Bones? Is it you?'

But no reply came. No sound other than the run of the water in the gullies and pools, the grating of pebbles and the surge of the tide.

The man's hand remained in the air and made a poor, feeble gesture, as if there were little strength left in it.

Good luck to ye, shipmate, it seemed to say. *Fair weather always, and safe sailing.*

'Good luck,' Tom whispered, so quietly, speaking only to his own ears and to the sound of the wind as it droned in the hollows of the rock.

Good luck, Mr Bones. Good luck.

The man lowered his hand, and he took up the

oars again, and he left the bottle there where it was in the sea. With an apparent resurgence of strength, he resumed his rowing and he propelled the boat straight out towards the sea, directly away from the land and out to where the marker buoy rang its eternal anthem of warning. He was headed straight for the destruction of the rocks, Tom realised. But he rowed on, reckless, heedless – like a man who has nothing left to lose.

Then the figure was gone, enveloped in darkness. Dark on dark. He and the night had blended into one. They were both impenetrable, unfathomable. As blank and unreadable as the far depths of the ocean.

Tom looked down. There was a phosphorescent glow at the shore line. Some minerals in the rocks gave off tiny stars of light. They twinkled, like fire-flies. The wind ruffled his hair. Everything felt calm now. Night had come and yet it felt like dawn and a new day. He took a last look out to sea. He couldn't see the bottle now. He didn't really expect to. The ebbing tide would have it. It would be on its way out towards the deep oceans and the shipping lanes that carried the cargoes of the world around the spinning globe.

He wished it safe journey and good speed. Though it didn't really have a destination. The journey was all it had.

190

He turned away from Needle Rock to take the coastal path, and he walked on home.

Tom was wrong, however, in his expectations. The sea did not carry the bottle away out to deep water. It became caught up in cross currents and undertows. It languished a while at slack water, and then, when the tide came back in, the bottle was carried in with it, back towards land. It missed the rocks and the harbour, and the ingoing surge bore it up into the estuary and towards Rose Haven. It floated along past the ferry point. But Gareth didn't see it. Then, when the tide changed again, it got trapped in some shallows and was becalmed. It was locked in the estuary, just like the big ships at anchor and the snarled driftwood by the riverbanks. For now, there it remained, far from the swell of the sea.

20

EMBARKING

'They're sailing out next week,' Gareth said. 'Both of them. *Ocean Emerald* and *Ocean Pearl*. Off together.'

It was back and forth time again. Tom was helping out on the ferry. Things weren't too busy that Saturday. It wasn't peak high season yet. But come the mid-summer and the tourists, the cars would be queuing for hours, backed up for a mile or more, waiting to get on to the ferry.

'How do you know?' Tom asked.

'We get advance warning,' Gareth said. 'We can't run the ferry when they're coming out of the haven. Don't want them smashing into us, do we, Tom?'

'Why can't they go out at night, when there's no one around?'

'They can if the tide's right, but it's not at present. Shouldn't take more'n an hour though. Come and watch them leave if you want. Next Sunday – a week tomorrow. But get here early.'

'Yes, I will,' Tom said. 'I'd like to see that. Will there be tugs towing them out?'

'First off, yes,' Gareth said. 'A bit of a pull and a shove'll help get them going.'

Tom looked at the two giant ships at anchor. Those men were still at work on the *Ocean Pearl*. The cradle was low again, down near the waterline.

'Haven't they finished their painting?'

'Almost, I reckon,' Gareth said. 'Looks like they're nearly done. Be all wrapped up by next week, anyway. Have to be, if they're off soon.'

'I wonder where they're going,' Tom said, a part of him wishing that he could be on board and go with them.

'Who knows?' Gareth said. 'Somewhere far away. Pacific, Indian Ocean, South China Sea . . .'

Tom looked up to the horizon. What romance, what adventure, what possibility, he thought, was in those names.

'Must be great to go to places like that, don't you think, Uncle Gareth?'

Gareth gave his nephew a curious glance. It was not altogether one of approval.

'I think you've got a bit of somebody else in you, Tom, boy,' he said. 'I think there's a bit of your dad in you. He was always hankering after far off places and wanting to see the world.'

He didn't say any more. But his thoughts were implicit. If Tom's father hadn't hankered after the sight

193

of far off places, he might still be here today. As Gareth was. Going back and forth across the estuary. Those who took the risks paid the price sometimes. But did that mean, Tom wondered, that the risks weren't worth taking?

Maybe he did have some of his dad in him. And maybe he was proud of that.

He looked inland at the big ships. The men in the cradle were nearing the end of their long, interminable labour. The hull was nearly covered in fresh, grey paint – only a few days' work remaining. Tom would definitely come to see the big ships leave. It would be something special to watch those two massive vessels head out for the ocean, like two great whales taking off on their migratory paths.

The two men were still there working, long after Tom had set off for home. They worked all of the next day, and into the Monday too. Then all the crew members began to get the ship ready for its departure on the coming Sunday.

When Tom returned to Delwick that evening, he spotted Stovey at the harbour wall. His row boat was back in the water, repairs completed, and it was tied up by his dinghy. He was surrounded by crab and lobster pots, examining them for defects and patching them up.

Tom wheeled his bike over to where Stovey was at

work. The old fisherman looked up and gave him a nod.

'All right, boy,' he said. 'How's it going?'

But Tom wasn't in the mood for how's it going and small talk like that. He needed to know one thing, and one thing only. The question had rankled with him. It made no sense to ask it, yet he had to be told. He needed that confirmation.

'Stovey,' he said. 'Are you Ted Bones?'

Stovey stared at him.

'Am I *who*?'

'You've got to tell me the truth, Stovey. Is it you who finds the bottles and sends the replies to the messages?'

'You w*hat*?'

'Stovey, you've got to tell me the truth. It's important. Are you Ted Bones?'

Stovey didn't seem to know whether to be outraged or amused. He settled for perplexed.

'And who's Ted Bones, when he's at home then?' he said.

'Stovey, I'm not a kid any more. And none of it's funny.'

'None of what's funny? What're you on about?'

'Look, if it's a joke, Stovey, you have to tell me. It's all right if it is. I can get over it and it doesn't matter. But I have to know.'

Stovey gave him a weighing-up look, of contemplation and slow assessment.

'Tom, I don't know what this is about, but you can rest assured that whoever Ted Bones is, he isn't Dave Stovey. You've got my word on that.'

Tom held his gaze.

'Is that true?'

Stovey grimaced.

'Tom, boy, if this goes on much longer, you and me are going to fall out.'

Tom looked away. He believed him. Which meant that . . .

'I'm sorry,' he said. 'I just had to ask.'

'What's going on with you, Tom?' Stovey said. 'What's this all about?'

'It's nothing,' Tom said. 'It doesn't matter. I can't tell you. I can't tell anyone.' Then he paused and added. 'There's nobody to tell anyway. Nobody else would understand.'

He abruptly turned and wheeled his bike away.

'Tom!' Stovey called after him. 'Tom! What's this about? Aren't we friends any more? What's up with you?'

Tom didn't look back. He kept going. In truth, he didn't even hear what Stovey said. His mind was somewhere else.

The week went by. Saturday came. Normally Tom would go to the ferry to help Gareth but he changed his regular days around. The ships were leaving Rose Haven first thing on Sunday, so he'd be at the estuary early tomorrow morning. Besides, his mother wanted him to look after the shop today while she got on with some work. The tourist season was fast approaching and she wanted to increase her stock – which meant she had to make it, and preferably without interruption.

At Rose Haven the ships were all but ready. Arrangements had been made for tugboats to come around the coast to hook up to the big ships and take them out of the estuary into the open sea. There were no tugs berthed in Delwick harbour; they'd have to come from one of the bigger ports nearby, from Plymouth or Penzance.

The painters' cradle still dangled down the side of the *Ocean Pearl* on that final Saturday. The two men in it, down at the waterline, were putting the very last touches to their work. Keo, the Cambodian, was glad the job was ended and happy to be soon on his way. He had been at sea for over a year and hadn't seen his family in all that time. He'd be glad to be moving on. All the same, he wondered if he might acquire a souvenir or two before he left. Maybe there'd be time for a quick visit into the nearby village. He could pick something up there, some memento of his travels.

'You okay, Charlie?'

The other man in the cradle nodded. The deep scar on his head had healed, but many other things had not. He owed his life to Keo, who had pulled him from the water. The skipper had been against it, but Keo had insisted. Stopping to get a man out of the water meant time lost. It could take hours to stop a ship that size, send a dinghy out, effect a rescue, then once again get underway. Time was money and the captain was under pressure from the ship owners to always keep moving, to arrive on time, pick up another cargo. Besides, it could have been something else in the water, not a man at all, but just a piece of flotsam.

Ships didn't always stop to pick up those who needed to be rescued. Life was cheap. Cargo was expensive.

As they finished their work, Keo noticed something in the water, drifting towards them.

'Hey, Charlie!'

He pointed. Charlie looked and saw the bottle bobbing alongside. It was green and it was glass and it was just a bottle. One more piece of rubbish, floating in the water no doubt. But then again you never knew. You could find interesting things in unpromising places. A sailor wasn't a sailor who had no curiosity about the offerings of the sea.

'Hey, Charlie! Something inside. You hold on!'

Charlie watched as Keo took a boat hook that lay

in the cradle and attempted to bring the bottle in towards them. But he couldn't reach. Charlie went to take the boat hook from him, for he was the taller, with a longer reach.

'You be careful, Charlie. You don't want to fall in . . .'

Charlie didn't say anything. He didn't say much. He never did. But he took the hook, reached out, and guided the bottle over. Then he lay on the cradle, extended his arm, and plucked it from the water.

'Hey, you got it, Charlie.'

Charlie handed Keo the bottle. He put the boat hook back down, out of the way, everything stowed neatly – the sailor's way.

Keo unscrewed the bottle top and prised out a tube of paper from inside.

'There a letter, Charlie. You see?'

Keo opened the letter up, but he couldn't really read it. He had some spoken English, which he had picked up from his travels as he had gone along, but he had never learned it formally. He handed the paper over.

'You read it, Charlie. What it say?'

Charlie took the paper and studied it. It seemed to be an effort for him to read what was there, as if the blow he had suffered to his head had not only cost him his memory of people and events, but had taken away his ability to read and to understand.

He mouthed the words as he read them, and as he did, the familiarity of language came back. It was okay. He could read it. Once started, it wasn't any trouble.

'What's it say, Charlie? What the message say?'

Keo didn't get an answer. The big man beside him just went on reading the letter, over and over. He would get to the end of it and then he would immediately start again. Over and over. His eyes scanned the page, got to the last line, went back to the beginning.

'What's it say, Charlie? What the letter say? It good news, Charlie? It good news?'

But his companion didn't answer. At length, he let his hand, which held the letter, fall to his side. Keo looked at him, worried, concerned.

'What's up, Charlie? You bad again? What's up, Charlie? You okay?'

Still the other man didn't answer. He just went on staring. His face was deeply tanned and yet the colour appeared to have gone from it. He looked as if he had seen a ghost.

200

21

AFTER MANY DAYS . . .

The day had been relatively quiet and the shop not particularly busy. But Tom had sold a few pieces – three jugs, two teapots, a vase and two plates. He would turn the sign in the window around soon, then count up the money and take it in to where his mother was working, applying a final coat of lacquer to some of her finer and more expensive designs.

It was with slight annoyance that he heard the clatter of the gate outside, because he was keen to close the shop. He was a bit peckish now. He wanted to lock up and get into the kitchen and find something to eat. He should have flipped that Open sign round to Closed a bit sooner.

Here they came. He could hear footsteps in the courtyard. Another couple of tourists, probably. He'd have to be polite to them, smile and be patient as they browsed around.

He looked up as the door opened and was surprised to see a small, dark-complexioned man walk somewhat hesitantly into the shop. He smiled as he entered, and

201

as he did, he held the door open for another man who followed behind him.

'This it, Charlie?' the smaller man said. 'This the place?'

Tom watched as the second man came in. He looked around. He stared at all the pots and plates and mugs and vases. And then his eyes rested on Tom. Tom returned his gaze. He held it, and then he slowly got to his feet, and then he ran. For what he saw he could not dare believe. So he ran for all he was worth. He ran from the shop and across the cobbled yard and into the workshop where his mother sat at a table, a brush in her hand, painting an intricate floral design upon a bowl.

'Mum . . . !'

'Tom!' She snapped at him in irritation as the crash of the opening door startled her and caused her to jerk the brush and smudge the paint. 'Tom, don't you know better than to . . .'

'Mum. Mum. In the shop!'

'What?'

'Mum. In the shop. People in the shop.'

'Yes, well, so? Just deal with it. You've done it before. Just wrap up what they want and take the money.'

'Mum . . . Mum . . .'

'What? Tom, what's wrong with you? What is it?'

202

'Mum, in the shop . . .'

'What?'

'It's Dad,' he said. 'It's Dad.'

She stood up. The brush fell from her hand. The bowl toppled and smashed upon the floor. It was in her mind to yell at him, to say, 'Tom, don't be stupid. How can you even say a thing like that . . . ?'

But something in his eyes, in his face, in his reaching hand that grasped for hers – something quelled her anger before it arose.

'Tom . . .'

'In the shop, Mum. In the shop . . . You've got to come . . .'

His hand was in hers and he was dragging her to come with him, he was bearing her away, like the outgoing tide. She followed, her steps quickening as they went, until the two of them were clattering over the stones of the yard, and they were inside the shop, with the smell of pottery and glaze around them. And there were two men, one small and dark, the other tall and bearded, with a deep brutal scar upon his forehead.

'This them, Charlie? This your boy, Charlie? This your missus?'

Tom's mother was still holding his hand, her grip like iron, her nails digging deep.

'Run and get your sister, Tom. Run and get Marie . . .'

'Mum . . .'

'Run and get Marie.'

He didn't need telling a third time. He ran. He crashed through the door and pounded up the stairs and into his sister's room.

'Marie!'

'How dare you come in here without knocking! How dare you barge into my room like that, you little . . .'

The insult never left her lips. She saw his eyes, his face, his hand reaching out for her as it had reached for his mother's hand.

'Marie . . . you've got to come, you've got to come . . .'

She went with him, swiftly, her steps light on the stairs.

'What is it, Tom? Who is it? What is it, Tom? Who's come? Who's here? Tom . . .'

Across the yard. Inside the door. There they were now, there they all were. And the small, dark man, with such a smile on his face.

'This your daughter, Charlie? This your girl? She very pretty, Charlie. She like my girl. Both very pretty.'

Tom saw something that he had not noticed before.

In his father's right hand was a scrap of paper, in the other a dark green bottle. Its surface was scratched and scraped and weathered in an unusual way. Tom

204

knew it. How could he not? He had thrown it himself into the sea. He had written a message and rolled it up and had put it in that bottle and sealed it tight. He had cast his bread upon the waters. And now, and now . . . it had come back to him, after many days.

His father saw him staring at the scratched, green glass.

'This is how I remembered everything,' he said. 'This is what brought it back to me. I found the bottle . . . I found this message, and it all came back . . .'

He handed the letter to Tom's mother. She held it and read it silently. Tom knew it by heart.

We all miss you and always will. I wish we had a place to visit, but we don't. Only the sea. So the sea is the place I always go to, and I write letters to it, and somehow, it writes back, even though it says things that I can't believe.

Anyway, this is just to let you know that we think of you always and you will never be forgotten . . .

This bottle might sail around the world for ever, I guess. But that won't matter, as it will always be there to remind me of you. It will be like a memorial – at least that's how I see it. My memorial in the sea.

I think of you often and I always will. I'll

205

*never forget you as long as I live. If I wrote
everything I feel, Dad, I would fill a thousand
bottles. I don't think there's room for all I feel
and all I have to say. There aren't enough bottles
in the world, Dad, or enough bits of paper.*

Bye, Dad.

Love for ever . . .

Nobody said a word. They were too full for words
and could think of none. All the words in the world
seemed too meagre. All that wealth and richness of
expression that had filled a million books with a thousand shades of meaning – there was still nothing
adequate. There was nothing a word could manage
that an embrace could not accomplish an infinite
number of times better. And they discovered as much
as they held each other, entangled, mute, indivisible,
like something shattered made whole again, rendered
perfect and complete.

Keo seemed the only one with anything to say.

'So – we all back together, huh? Everybody happy
now, Charlie? Everybody happy?'

Finally somebody answered him.

'Yes, Keo,' Samuel Pellow said. 'Everybody happy
now. Thank you. Thanks to you . . .'

'Maybe I buy a pot,' Keo said. 'For souvenir.'

Once they had heard his story, they would have

given him all the pots and souvenirs in the world.

Yes, Keo had saved Samuel Pellow, but it was Tom who had found him. For although what is lost cannot always be recovered, some stubborn, unreasonable individuals go on clinging to hope, long after it is sensible to do so. They are usually disappointed. But sometimes . . . just sometimes . . .

'I didn't give up, did I, Marie?' Tom said to her later. 'I didn't, did I? I didn't give up. Even when everyone else had, I didn't give up.'

To his surprise, the answer she gave him was a kiss.

22

ONE MORE MESSAGE, AFTER ALL

Dear Mr Bones,

Thank you for your last letter.

I don't know if you will ever get this, but I am just sending it to say that you were right. The person I was asking about was here all along, but we had good reason to think otherwise.

It seems that when the ship he was on sank in the storm, when its cargo shifted in the hold and made it roll, he was not inside, but on the upper deck, and was thrown into the sea. But it was a long way from the deck to the surface of the water, and when he fell he was struck unconscious. His head was hit by something in the water, and he was only saved by two other crewmen who were also thrown from the ship to the sea.

They had managed to release one of the life rafts and they pulled him on board. He was in a coma for two or three days he thinks, and when he regained consciousness, he did not know where he was or who he was any more.

The survivors drifted for a long time, thinking that somebody would come to save them, but they never did. The two other people on the life raft did not survive and he had to bury them at sea so there was only him left and then he began to run out of food and water and started to become unconscious again.

Finally he was rescued by a big cargo boat. The captain did not want to stop, but the crew got him to and the person I am talking about was saved. Only he didn't have any memory or know who he was, and so no one knew where he belonged or where to take him, so he just stayed on board and he seemed to know all about boats and what to do, so they kept him on as a member of the crew. He got to make some friends there, and someone in particular was very kind and looked after him and named him Charlie.

The ship he was on sailed all over the world and changed captains and called in at several ports, but he could never go off the ship as he didn't have a passport any more or any of the right papers and didn't even know who he was. So he just stayed on board and did maintenance work and things like that.

The ship was called the Ocean Pearl, and eventually it ran out of cargoes to carry for a while, and so it was laid up in a haven along with its sister ship, the Ocean Emerald. *They were both about to set sail again when this person I was asking you about, Samuel Pellow, found something in the water – a sort of message, a bit like this one – inside a bottle, just like this one too. And when he opened it up and read it, he discovered it was from his son, who is me. The message brought everything back to him, and he could remember who he was and where he had come from once more. And when he looked around him, he realised that it did not just look familiar, as he had always thought, but was familiar, and it was somewhere he had known all his life, and it was home.*

So you were right, you see, Mr Bones. There wasn't anyone in Davy Jones's Locker by the name of Samuel Pellow, as he was here all along. Which is good news, as you can imagine, and we are all very pleased about that. So I am sorry if I wasted your time.

But, you know something, Mr Bones . . . I don't know . . . I don't know if I really believe in you, to tell the truth. I sometimes suspect that you are not Mr Ted Bones at all. I half suspect that you are Mr Dave Stovey instead, who somehow found the messages that I put into the sea, and just wanted to be kind and to give some faint hope to your correspondent – myself. And yet, if he did that, I don't understand how. So maybe you are Mr Bones after all.

So I don't know what to think, to be honest. For, though I have confronted Mr Stovey and have tried to have things out with him, he swears he doesn't know anything about anything. But then, he would say that, wouldn't he?

Of course, if he is right, well . . . then you must be a ghost, Mr Bones, and that is who I am writing to. I am writing to a ghost, to someone who died a long, long time ago. If so, then you are a very kind ghost, Mr Bones, and I hope that you will rest easy down in the Locker, along with all the other sailors of far away and long ago.

I don't think there is much more for me to say now, Mr Bones, except to say thank you again and to say cheerio and goodbye.

It's funny how things turn out, isn't it? If I had never written to the sea, well, my last message might never have been found, and Samuel Pellow might never have found it and got his memory back. He would have sailed away on the Ocean Pearl once more, and we might never have seen him again, ever, and have gone on believing that he was down in the Locker, with you and all the others.

211

So I suppose that it does no harm, does it, Mr Bones, to cast your bread upon the waters, as people say? After all, what is there to lose? For you never know, do you – what things may come your way?

Bye then, Mr Bones. I expect I will see you one day – if you are Mr Ted Bones and not old Stovey playing his tricks. I suppose we all end up in Davy Jones's Locker, or somewhere else like that, eventually. But hopefully not for a long time yet.

I'll finish now. This is the longest message I have ever written, and I hope it will all fit in the bottle – or maybe I'll need an extra large one.

Bye, Mr Bones – or Stovey, if it's you.

Thanks for writing to me.

Your pen and bottle friend,

Tom Pellow. Son of Samuel Pellow.

x

Tom

Alone by the Smokestack, Tom took aim and threw the bottle long and far into the sea. He had thought that he had already written his last message, but circumstances had proved him wrong, and had demanded that he inscribe one further and final word.

This was the last, he decided. This definitely was the last.

He watched the bottle drift away from the land. The sun was high and the sky was bright and clear. It wasn't a time of mist and darkness; it wasn't a time for dark-clad figures to appear from nowhere, rowing out from the fog. It was all too fine and sparkling a summer's day for anything of that kind.

The current took the bottle. The tide ran out with it, taking it along past the headland, past the marker buoy and the bell, and then out to mid-water and into the Atlantic. It wasn't seized by any eddies or undertows this time. No mid-water streams swirled it back in towards land, or sucked it into the estuary waters, then up past the *King Billy* ferry and into the peace and silence of Rose Haven.

It drifted on out to the open sea. Great ships sailed past it – cargo ships, warships, factory ships, huge trawlers, oil tankers, cruise liners, boats of all kinds.

The bottle bobbed on – tiny in the ocean, just a fragment, a speck of dust.

Rose Haven was empty. The *Ocean Emerald* and the *Ocean Pearl* were long gone. The *King Billy* ferry chugged and clanked back and forth across the river. You'd have thought its skipper would have gone mad by now – from the sheer boredom of making the same short journey over and over, again and again. But no. He seemed quite sane and cheerful. He even whistled as he worked.

The bottle bobbed on still. It was deep into the main shipping lanes now. Another current took it, and carried it south. The water around it grew warmer. Exotic fish swam underneath it; an albatross flew above. But on it went.

In time the water grew colder. There was ice. Eyes stared at it from an ice floe – curious penguins, all black and white, like waiters in their formal suits. The bottle drifted on. More ice formed; the bottle was held in its grasp. A long winter passed, and then the thaw and the bottle moved again and drifted onwards, going north now, and then east.

It journeyed on, along the coast of South America, to the Cape of Good Hope, up the eastern coast of Africa, then, in time, up around Newfoundland and into Arctic waters. A paw swatted at it. A big white paw. But the polar bear missed it, so the bottle again drifted on. The bear turned its attention to a passing seal. The water chilled. Ice held it again for a while.

The years have gone by now. Tom Pellow is grown up, tall and strong, and he works as a merchant seaman, just as his father once did. Though Samuel Pellow long since gave up the sea. His wife, Alison, still makes pots and vases. There's the new tea shop in the tourist season too, and so they make a living. Marie Pellow is a teacher, and works abroad.

214

Old Stovey is dead now. His ashes – as he wanted them to be – were scattered upon the sea. There he rests, down in Davy Jones's Locker, with all the other mariners from centuries past.

The ice thaws. The bottle resumes its journey. One day someone might find it. It may wash up on some sandy beach, overlooked by palms and coconut trees. Or maybe it will drift in to some coral shore. Or a child with a bucket and spade in hand will spot it bobbing in the water, and run down to fetch it, excited and triumphant, bringing it back to where the rest of the family lounge on towels and in deckchairs, crying, 'Look what I've found! See what I've got! It's a message! A message in a bottle!'

Finally, after all its years of travelling, the bottle will be opened, and the message read.

It's hard to know what anyone will make of it.

'What does that mean?' they'll say, quite perplexed. Or they'll quickly dismiss it out of hand. 'It's just someone, having a joke!'

Or maybe the bottle will drift on for ever, until the oceans all run dry and the earth falls into the sun.

Sometimes at night, Tom Pellow stands on the bridge of the great ship of which he is now the captain. He takes up his binoculars and looks out into the night, at the darkness and the black waters.

215

He fancies he sees something out there sometimes. A bottle. Or a glimmer of light.

Sometimes, somebody asks him what he might be looking for, and why he stares so intently out into the night.

Just searching for a glimpse, he says, of old Ted Bones. Then he gives a wry smile. No one knows what on earth he is talking about. And he never makes any effort – or feels any need – to explain.